A Family Affair

by Frank Sol

Chapter One

Well, I certainly do know how to pick a winner.

Why the hell does every single one of my relationships seem to be destined for disaster? Samantha, Mary, Elizabeth...every last damn one has crashed and burned.

I mean, I certainly do alright for myself in other areas. I have a great job, working at one of the local "Big Five" banks. No, I don't work as a teller; I'm one of the guys who works behind-the-scenes, keeping everything flowing smoothly on the I.T. end. The salary is not spectacular, but it's more than enough to allow me to rent my own apartment, keep a decent car, party it up a bit, and all that sort of thing. It certainly puts me above the average twenty-three year-old.

However, when it comes to relationships, forget it. Every single one always goes badly in the end. Sophia is only the latest in my unbroken string....

Sophia dumped me earlier this evening.

Well, she didn't exactly dump me, but we had a fairly public screaming match which ended with her telling me to go and fuck myself and never come near her again, which I guess amounts to the same thing as being dumped.

It's for the best really, or so I tried to console myself as I drove down the street. To tell the whole truth, I don't think Sophia was really all that interested in me as a person. Hell, I knew she wasn't interested in me.

What she was really after was my bank balance.

As long as I was buying her nice presents and taking her out to clubs and things like that, she was happy. It was a shallow relationship between two extremely shallow people. Yes, it was long past time that I faced up to the bitter truth. I knew how things stood between us. I knew she couldn't give a damn about me and, if I'm honest—which I really did owe it to myself to be—I felt pretty much the same about her.

Honestly, I let things continue for as long as they did because Sophia was a real looker. A Greek goddess straight from Olympus. When she was dressed to kill, everyone noticed, and having her with me gave me one hell of a boost. How shallow is that?

We'd had fights before, of course. What couple doesn't have fights? They usually happened when Sophia didn't get her own way about something. In the end I'd give her what she wanted and everything would go smoothly again.

This time, though, it was different. This time it was really over.

This particular trouble started a few days ago when I went round to Sophia's house to pick her up and found out that she'd already left. Her mother was home and invited me in. Like a complete moron, I accepted the invitation. Helena had obviously decided that she wanted a taste of the sort of life her daughter was enjoying, and the woman practically threw herself at me. I suppose, for a forty year-old, she was quite attractive. But I'm not into older women, period. I tried to point this out to her in a nice way, but she was having none of it.

As soon as she was sure that she had no chance with me I suddenly became a pervert who was only interested in young girls. Suddenly Sophia was an innocent little seventeen-year-old, and I had used my money to brainwash her into going out with me. Innocent? Yeah whatever. Sophia had told me herself that she had lost her v-card at twelve and had been screwing around ever since then. Anyway, the scene was rapidly turning ugly so I came to the conclusion that the best thing was to get of there, and quick. I decided it was probably best not to mention this little scenario to Sophia. However, her mother was obviously not happy about me repelling her advances, and if she couldn't have me, then neither could her dear little Sophia. When I stopped by the house to collect the girl earlier this evening, she almost gouged my eyes out. She was blazing mad, accusing me of trying to get it on with her mother. I tried to put her right, telling her that it was really the other way around, but she refused to even listen. The fight got louder and louder, and then she physically came at me, her hand flying at me face. Those bloody nails of hers could have done serious damage. Luckily, all I got was a couple of scratches. That's when I decided I didn't want to hang around any longer, and as I left she told me, in no uncertain terms, not to come back.

Yes, I think it's probably fair to say that me and Sophia are no longer an item.

Following our fight, I really needed a serious drink. I took the *BMW* home, quickly doctored up my damaged face, and then walked round to my local bar, which was just a couple of streets away.

"Hey, Eddie!"

I waved back at Mason, got myself a beer from the bartender, and headed to that table where Mason was sitting. I knew a few of the other people there, and I took one of the chicken wings as the platter made its round of the table.

"Early night?" Mason asked. "I thought you had a hot date."

"Sophia made other plans."

Mason laughed. "Had another fight?"

"A real doozey this time."

"Don't sweat it." Mason refilled his glass from the pitcher resting in the centre of the table. "There's plenty of chicks out there just waiting for a taste." The rest of the table quickly nodded their agreement with that.

"I've had more than just a taste."

"Yeah, well girls are like cars...the new model is always hotter than what you're currently driving." He drained his glass.

Even before I'd finished my first beer, it was readily becoming apparent that I really wasn't in the mood for socialising. The alcohol, instead of relaxing me, was simply only making me feel more depressed. "I'm just not in the mood for the bar tonight," I told Mason after hastily downing finishing my second. "I think I'm just gonna call it a night and head home."

Mason nodded. "Yeah, sometimes that's the best thing you can do." With his square jaw and blond surfer-style looks, he certainly never had any trouble landing himself a girl. He was currently eyeing a brunette in a low-cut tee-shirt.

"Good luck," I told him.

It was just a wild impulse for me to walk through the park; it isn't something I normally do. For one thing, it's not the safest place to wander alone after dark. But I needed to try to clear my head. It was a mild night and there was something therapeutic about walking through the darkness, looking up at the stars and realizing that, compared to the vastness of the universe, my own problems were fairly insignificant; I should mention that after a little alcohol I tend to become an amateur philosopher.

I'd only been walking for a few minutes when I noticed the crumpled heap lying across the path a short distance ahead of me. I'm almost ashamed to say that at this point my first reaction was to turn around and walk the other way; I had enough problems of my own without worrying about some drunk, passed out in the park. But my conscience got the better of me and I felt I had little choice but to make sure that the person was alright. I'd go and check, and if he was indeed a drunk, I'd leave him where he was to enjoy his temporary yet blissful release from this cruel and unforgiving world. Not just a philosopher but a poet as well; the small amount of beer I'd consumed really was working overtime this evening.

Cautiously I approached the shadowy heap. "You okay, buddy?"

There was no response.

Now my imagination kicked in, big time. Suppose this wasn't a drunk, but a dead body? *The last thing I needed at the moment was to get involved in a murder investigation.* I took a few tentative steps closer, telling myself not to be so stupid. *He won't be dead, just dead to the world.* "Hey, you okay, buddy?" I repeated.

This time there was a mumbled response, more of a grunt than anything else.

At least he was alive, I thought to myself. "You need any help or anything?" Stupid bloody question. Of course he needed help. *The real question was whether or not I was prepared to give it.*

"Leave me alone." Even though the muttered words were slurred, the message was clear enough.

Normally, under circumstances like these, I wouldn't need telling twice. However, there was something familiar about that voice. I remained frozen in my place, frowning as my mind spun. *How do I know that voice?* Then it came to me! "Marco?"

"Leave me alone," the figure repeated, an arm flopping out aimlessly.

Now I was almost sure. Sure enough to want to confirm my suspicions, anyway. I knelt over the figure to get a look at his face and managed a quick glimpse before I had to step back, reeling. "Christ, Marco, you stink." Trying to hold my breath so as not to inhale the foul mixture of odours rising from him, I again knelt down and rolled the figure over onto his back.

Yep, it was definitely Sophia's twin brother.

He groaned.

"Oh, shit!" I muttered as I saw the state he was in.

From the overwhelming smell of alcohol on his breath, he'd drunk himself almost into insensibility. Unfortunately, that wasn't all he'd done. There was vomit down the front of his grey hoodie and, from the strong smell of urine, it was reasonable to assume that he'd also pissed himself.

"Leave me alone," the boy repeated, his words barely understandable.

I turned my head away to draw in some clean air while I thought about the situation I was now in. "What the hell am I supposed to do with you?" I asked out loud. Leaving him laying on the ground was out of the question. The kid was only seventeen, and God knows what might happen to him if I simply went home and left him like this. "I suppose the easiest thing to do is to call 911 and let the cops them take care of you."

I left my cell-phone clipped to my belt though. I didn't like the idea of leaving him to the not-so-tender mercies of 'the city's finest'. *He'd certainly end up spending the night in the police cells, and would probably even get charged with something or other.* "I should drag you back home." That really would be the best thing to do with him...only I could think of a number of reasons not to do that. Firstly, he lived a good couple of miles away and obviously would never be able to walk there in this condition, and I certainly wasn't going to drive him in my nice car seeing as he was covered in piss and sick. Secondly, I had no desire to show my face round at their house at the moment. And thirdly, it was unlikely there would be anyone in anyway. Sophia would be out with her friends, no doubt telling them what a complete bastard I was, and her mother would be out on the prowl for herself; there was no father around.

"I'm just too damned soft-hearted," I grumbled aloud. "That's always been my trouble, Marco. Come on." I reached under his arms and, with a struggle, lifted him slowly into a standing position. "I'm gonna to have to take you home with me."

Since Marco showed no signs of being able to support himself, I had to almost carry him. Luckily he wasn't especially heavy; even though he was seventeen, he was extremely small for his age.

Slowly, and with a great deal of effort, we made the half-kilometre walk to my apartment. It was with great relief that I finally kicked the door closed behind me. That had to have been the longest half-kilometre of my life. It wasn't just the effort of dragging Marco, but also the smell, which I was sure was getting worse all the time. Almost exhausted, I hauled him the last few metres down the hallway into the bathroom, and then dumped him unceremoniously down onto the tiles.

Then I took a step back to get my first good look at him. If anything, the boy looked even worse than I had first imagined.

Marco sat there, his back propped against the side of the tub. His face was pale and his eyes flicked open and closed as if he didn't have full control over them.

An unpleasant thought occurred to me. "Marco, have you taken anything, or is this just from booze?"

"Leave me the hell alone."

"Marco, talk to me," I said, taking hold of his shoulders and shaking him. "Have you taken anything? Any pills or stuff?" I pushed the sleeve of his hoodie up past the elbow. There were no Marcos on his inner arm; not that I really knew what I was looking for, of course. Quickly I repeated the procedure on his other arm. At least it didn't look like he'd injected anything. "Have you taken any drugs?"

"Don't do drugs. Just drink. Now leave me the fuck alone."

Well, that's a relief. "So now I just have to decide what to do with you." I could leave him like this on my bathroom floor until he came to his senses and then send him on his way, or I could clean him up. It had to be the latter, for my sake as much as for his; the smell was awful. *I don't want my whole place to smell like this!* "Marco, I can't leave you like this. I'm going to put you in the bath, then I'll lend you some of my clothes. Is that okay?"

The boy raised his head and looked at me. "Edward." A silly grin spread over his face.

At least he recognizes me, I thought.

"Edward," he said again. Then the grin disappeared and he started to cry.

"Shit." *Now what was I supposed to do?* If it had been a girl, I would have tried to comfort her, maybe even put my arm around her; that's assuming, of course, she wasn't covered in sick. But what the hell do you do with a crying seventeen-year-old boy? "Erm, you alright, Marco?" I tried, feeling more uncomfortable by the moment.

He looked up at me, his face screwed up in that ugly way that people do when they cry, the tears forming streaks down his dirty face.

At a bit of a loss, I put my hand on his shoulder and gave it a squeeze. "You'll be alright. Let's get you cleaned up and then you'll feel a lot better."

I made a quick dash to the kitchen and grabbed a black garbage bag from the drawer. I had to have something to put his clothes in and I certainly wasn't about to attempt to wash them or anything like that. I'd tie them up in the bag and then it would be up to Marco what he did with them. My Good Samaritan streak was only going so far.

Back in the bathroom, Marco had slid down until he was now sprawled out on the tiled floor, laying on his back like a turtle. He was mumbling something, but it was impossible to make out what it was, and I doubt that it would have made sense anyway. I managed to get him sitting up again, and then pulled the hoodie up over his head. The dark green tee-shirt that he was wearing underneath followed it up, so I just pulled both of them off together and bundled the stinking garments into the garbage bag. The smell of vomit was as bad as ever and I realized that I now had some of it down my own shirt from when I had supported the boy on our staggering walk home.

"Damn it," I sighed to myself, and then pulled off my own polo shirt and tossed it aside. Only then did I turn my attention back to the drunk teenager. What I saw came as a bit of a shock. I've already mentioned that Marco was small for his seventeen years. However, now that he was bare-chested, I could see exactly how underdeveloped he really was. His baggy clothing had gone a long way towards covering up his thin frame. From the looks of him, a few good meals wouldn't go amiss. What shocked me the most, however, were the bruises.

Marco had dark bruises on both of his upper arms as though someone had gripped him and squeezed, digging in their fingers. There were also large bruises on the side of his chest; it looked like he'd been either punched or kicked at some time in the recent past.

I lifted my eyes to the boy's face to find him smiling once more. A small earring hoop hung from his right ear. His upper body swayed backwards and forwards as he looked up at me with what I can only describe as 'trusting' eyes under his bushy eyebrows. "You look like you've been having a rough time," I said, smiling back. "Have you been fighting with someone?"

He shook his head in a rather comical way. "I don't fight. I'm a good boy." The he gave a short giggle. His mood changes were certainly mercurial, though it was probably the after effects of everything he'd been drinking. Marco watched me as I pulled off his sneakers and then his socks. His socks went into the bag with the other clothes, though I threw his sneakers over towards the wall, out of the way; he'd need something to wear on his feet and it was extremely unlikely anything of mine would fit. "What're ya doin'?" the teen asked as my hands went to the zipper at the front of his baggy jeans.

"I'm taking these off."

"Why?"

"Because you need get in the bath and you can't get in with your pants on." I didn't bother to mention the fact that he'd pissed himself; I can be quite diplomatic when I need to be. I grimaced to myself as I fumbled with his zip, knowing I was getting his pee on my fingers. *I suppose there are worse things I can get on my hands.* The jeans followed the other clothes into the bag. This left Marco wearing just a pair of filthy and worn-out grey briefs.

Marco looked down at his underwear and ran his fingers across the front. "They're wet," he observed.

"Yeah, they sure are."

"Do I have to take them off?"

"I think you'd better."

The teen gave another giggle. "Don't look," he said. He took hold of his briefs at the sides and pushed down, though when he tried to lift his backside up off the floor, he toppled over. "Oops!" he laughed.

I gave a sigh.

Marco continued to laugh as I went to his assistance and pulled the briefs all the way off, touching them as little as possible as I dropped them into the bag. Quickly, I tied a knot in the top of the bag to keep in the smell and then hurriedly went to the sink to wash my hands. By the time I turned back to Marco, he'd curled up into a ball on the floor and looked like he was about to go to sleep.

"Not yet you don't," I said, pulling on his arm. "You can't go to sleep yet. Bath first, and then you can sleep."

"Don't want a bath," he muttered, ineffectually trying to free his arm from my grasp. "Want sleep."

I briefly considered letting him have his way, and just leaving him on the bathroom floor for the night. It would certainly be the easiest option.

But I knew from the condition he was in that he was going to feel like shit when he woke in the morning—I'd woken up in that position before—and spending the night dirty and stinking on a cold, hard bathroom floor was, if anything, likely to make him feel an awful lot worse. "Bath first," I insisted. "Come on, Marco. It'll only take a few minutes."

"Don't want to." The smile had now disappeared and he was starting to get awkward.

Changing my mind about the bath, I suddenly had a much better idea. I bent over and scooped him up, depositing him roughly into the empty bathtub. He gave a moan and put up a token struggle, but he was in the tub before he even realized what was happening. While he lay there, complaining, I freed the shower attachment from the wall and turned on the spray.

"Aaarghhhhh!" He let out a scream as cold water splashed down over his body. It seemed that he was no longer quite so sleepy after all.

Now it was my turn to laugh as he made a completely uncoordinated attempt to climb out of the bath, his arms thrashing wildly; this was the most life he'd shown since I'd found him. His struggling eased as the water warmed up, until he was lying there passively, allowing me to rinse him down.

I picked up the soap and handed it to him. "Here, rub that over yourself."

He looked at me blankly.

With a sigh, I leaned forwards and rubbed the soap across his chest. While I did this, he lay back in the tub, a picture of wide-eyed, trusting innocence. I moved the soap lower, onto his stomach, rinsing him as I went. "Open your legs," I instructed.

Obediently, he opened up his legs as far as he could within the confines of the bath tub, revealing an untidy bush of pubes, dick, and balls.

At this point I hesitated. Washing his upper body for him was one thing, but touching him down there was a whole different ball game, if you'll excuse the pun. I once more considered handing him the soap and getting him to do it himself, but just as quickly dismissed this idea as a waste of time. Instead I settled for directing the spray over his exposed groin area, washing it as well as I could without actually touching it.

At least this should clean him up enough, I thought. *He can do a more thorough job himself when he came to his senses.*

Marco was still giggling.

"That'll do for now," I announced, turning off the water.

Marco, made to get up, but slipped on the wet surface, banging his head. "Ow!" he exclaimed.

"Hold on a minute," I said, quickly putting my arm behind his shoulders and supporting him. "You okay? Did you hurt yourself?"

He blinked a couple of times and shook his head.

Getting him out of the tub was harder than getting him in, and wasn't helped by the fact he was now wet and slippery. Eventually, with a lot of pulling and very little help from him, I got him sitting up on the edge of the bath. He was swaying dangerously and I didn't dare let go of him in case he lost his balance again. Holding onto him with one hand, I dried him off as best I could with the other, running the towel over his slim chest and back and down over his arms and legs. Soon all that remained was the private region between his legs. Trying to get him to dry his own groin area proved fruitless, and by this point I was starting to get tired and more than a little irritable. "To hell with it then!" With my hand inside the towel, I rubbed it over his pubes, then his dick and his balls, and then leaned him forwards and reached around and dried his ass.

"You'll do," I said, draping the wet towel over the rail. "Now let's sort out where you're sleeping."

"Need to pee," he said, the words coming out as little more than a mumble. He looked up at me with those big trusting eyes.

"Shit!" I muttered, looking up at the ceiling and counting to ten. I was starting to wish I'd left him where he was. Though even as I had this thought, I knew I didn't mean it. Even in this condition, there was something about Marco that I couldn't help but like. "Hold onto it a minute. You make a mess on my bathroom floor and I'll put you out of the door exactly as you are."

He gave another little giggle as though his drunken mind found this idea rather amusing.

I helped him over to the toilet and sat him down on the seat. "Right, go ahead and pee." I held onto his shoulders, just to make sure he didn't fall over, at the same time praying that he didn't do anything else. The idea of standing here holding him while he took a crap was one that I didn't care to dwell on.

"Done," he said.

I let him sit there a little longer, just to be sure, and then half-dragged, half-carried him through to my bedroom, where I dumped him onto my queen-sized bed. "Don't get too comfortable," I warned. "That one's mine. I'll sort something else out for you."

I did have a small guest room, but decided against putting Marco in there. If he was to be ill in the night, I wanted to be on hand to deal with it. Instead, I dragged the single mattress from the guest bed into my own bedroom and threw a sheet and duvet over it. "You can manage on this. It's certainly better than that path in the park."

Marco was sprawled out on his back, apparently already asleep. He was, of course, still completely naked, and I wondered whether to root out a pair of boxer shorts for him. Though getting them on him would be a struggle, and if he needed the toilet again in the night, he would be a lot easier to deal with as he was.

"I'll leave him then."

He moaned and complained as I dragged him from my bed and then dropped him, somewhat roughly, onto the mattress, but once in place he immediately settled down and appeared to be asleep again almost straight away.

"Goodnight, Marco," I grinned, as I looked down at his sleeping form. I stripped down to my silk shorts, made a quick visit to the bathroom, and then gratefully climbed into my own bed.

Chapter Two

I awoke with a headache pounding behind my temples.

I must have had more to drink the previous evening than I'd thought. Oh well, at least it was Saturday, which meant I wasn't due into work until after lunch. I gave a start at a moaning sound coming from behind me. "What the hell?" It was then that I recalled my involuntary guest. With a groan, I rolled over, away from the wall, and forced myself up out of bed to check on my unexpected guest.

It looked like Marco was still asleep; not that I could see much of him, since only the very top of his head was visible from under the duvet.

"Marco, you still alive?" I asked, smiling to myself, as I poked the duvet, roughly in the vicinity of where his shoulder would be.

There was soft moan, followed by a muffled "leave me alone".

"C'mon Marco, let's see what sort of condition you're in this morning." I peeled the top of the duvet back to reveal the boy's face. "Jesus! You look rough." This was an understatement.

The teen's face was pale with a greenish tinge and the black patches around his eyes would have put a panda to shame. Marco blinked up at me with a complete lack of comprehension on his face. "Edward?" he groaned after a long silence. "What the hell...where am I?"

"You're in my bedroom," I told him. "When I found you last night you were pretty far gone, and it was the easiest thing to bring you back here."

He looked confused for a moment, then dropped his head back, his eyes closing, as if trying to work it all out was just too much trouble. "I'm dying," he croaked.

I tried to stop myself from grinning and failed. "I'll get you a couple of Tylenol and a glass of water. It won't stop you dying, but it might help you feel a bit more comfortable while you do it."

"Urgh!" He rolled over, and clutched at his stomach.

"What's the matter?" I asked, expecting the worst.

"I think I'm gonna throw up."

Just as I'd suspected. I hastily grabbed his arm, hauling him to his feet. "Not in my bedroom you don't. Let's get you to the bathroom."

I managed to get him to his feet and started dragging him towards the open door, at which point he suddenly realized that he was naked, and reached back for the duvet. "No time to worry about that," I snapped. "You throw up in here and you're the one who's going to have to clean it up."

By the time I got him out of the bedroom and into the bathroom he was already retching and had his hand pressed tightly over his mouth. He lunged for the toilet, dropping to his knees in front of it. I left him to it.

I was in my kitchen, still dressed only in my silk boxers, making toast and coffee, when Marco resurfaced. He'd wrapped a bathtowel around his waist and stood in the kitchen doorway, holding onto the door frame as though it were the only thing keeping him upright.

"How're you feeling?" I asked, trying to hide my amusement and look suitably sympathetic. *It's been years since I drank myself into that bad of a condition.* But I remembered doing once or twice back in college.

"Like I died," he groaned. "Where are my clothes?"

"Did you see that black trash bag in the bathroom?"

"Yeah?"

"Well that's where your clothes are. Believe me, the way you are feeling at the moment, opening that bag would not be good idea."

"Why, what have you done to them?"

"Don't look at me, buddy. It wasn't me who threw up all down your front and pissed in your jeans."

"Oh shit!" He looked mortified.

"Don't worry about it," I said. "Come and sit down before you fall down." I indicated one of the kitchen chairs and he made his slow, and careful way over to it.

"So you...undressed me?"

"Yep. Someone had to sort you out and clean you up."

"You mean you washed me?" he asked, looking even more mortified.

I gave him a grin. "You really don't remember any of it do you? Mind you, I'm not surprised, considering the state you were in last night."

I placed a couple of Tylenol tablets and a large glass of orange juice on the table in front of him. "Here, take these. Drink the juice slowly and try to keep it down."

"I don't want it."

"Drink it anyway. You need the liquid inside you. Listen to the voice of reason...and of past experience. You need it."

He looked up at me, his head supported on his hands. "Did I say anything last night?" He blinked his eyes.

"About what?"

He looked embarrassed. "About anything at all?"

"Nothing that made any sense," I said, shaking my head. "You did quite a lot of giggling." I decided not to mention the crying. I took a bite of my toast and he pulled a face and looked away, lowering his head back onto his arms. "Don't you dare throw up in my kitchen," I warned.

I finished my own breakfast, then had a quick shower, and put a fresh shirt and pants on. I tossed last night's polo shirt into the laundry bag. When I returned to the kitchen Marco was still in the same position at the table. The Tylenol were gone and he'd managed about half of the glass of orange juice, but there was no other sign that that he'd moved at all since I'd left him.

"Do you want to go back to bed for a little while?" I suggested, taking pity on him. "Then you can get up again in an hour or so and have a shower. I'll lend you some clothes to put on."

He raised his head just far enough so that he could look at me. "Yeah, I think so," he said, gratefully.

"Do you want to ring your mother or anything first?" I asked, as he slowly got to his feet.

He froze in mid-step. "Why? She wouldn't care."

"If you say so," I shrugged. I followed him as he tentatively made his way back to the bedroom. He really was in a state; such is the price of too much boozing.

When he reached the mattress he sheepishly glanced back at me, then, removing the towel from his waist, he climbed back under the duvet.

It was coming up to lunchtime when I next went to check on him. Once again, all that was visible was a lump under the duvet. "Time to get up, Marco," I called.

There was, predictably, no response. "Come on, it's almost lunch time and I have to leave for work straight after lunch; I want you out of here before then. If you're going to get a shower and get cleaned up you need to be moving now."

There was a muffled a groan and what sounded like "I don't want to."

"Tough." I reached down and took hold of a corner of the duvet, yanking it away. "I haven't got time to mess around, so get yourself up."

"What the hell you doing?" he complained, curling himself into a ball, but not fast enough to hide his rampant erection. He glared up at me.

"I'm getting you up," I said, grinning at his discomfort. *Too be young again.* "Come on, Marco. I was good enough to let you stay here, and

I even let you have an extra couple of hours in bed, so don't mess me about now. If you're not in the bathroom in thirty seconds I'm going to tip a bowl of cold water on you." That was, of course, a total bluff, but he couldn't be sure that I wasn't serious.

"Can't I stay here while you go to work?"

"Not on your life."

He muttered something under his breath and rolled onto his stomach before reaching for the towel that he had discarded earlier. He tried to keep his back to me as he wrapped the towel around himself, but there was no hiding the prominent bulge in the front of the towel as he passed me on his way to the bathroom.

While Marco showered, I sorted out some clothes for him. He was much smaller than me, so anything I lent him would be far too big. Though most of the teenagers these days seem to wear stuff like that anyway, so he wouldn't exactly look out of place.

He finally reappeared about ten minutes later. He was still only wearing the towel, but drops of water on his chest and shoulders indicated that he'd had the shower. He did look much better than he had earlier that morning, and he even managed a sort of shy smile.

"How you feeling now?" I asked.

"Rough," he admitted. "But not quite as bad as earlier."

"If you get yourself into the sort of condition you were in last night, you're going to have to pay for it. Was that a one-off or a regular thing?"

He shrugged.

"Sorry," I said. "None of my business. Though it's not a good idea to go and pass out in the park. There are all sorts of weirdos out there at night." I indicated the small piles of clothing I'd placed on the edge of my bed. "Here, I've found you something to wear."

"Thanks." As he passed me to get to the clothes I again noted the bruises on his upper arms and chest. "You look like you've been involved in some rough stuff."

He immediately froze, his face reddening. "It's nothing," he muttered, not looking at me.

"Okay, if you say so." I can take a hint; this was quite obviously something he didn't want to talk about. "I'll be out in the kitchen. Would you like something to eat before you go?"

Marco shook his head. "Don't talk about food," he said, his hand going to his mouth.

I hid a smile. I knew just how he felt. *Yep, I've been there.*

When Marco appeared in the kitchen a few minutes later he looked like a typical teenager. I was right about the oversized tee-shirt and sweatpants not looking too out of place. "Feel's funny, wearing someone else's clothes," he said.

"Well, if you prefer, you could always get your own out of the bin-bag. Make sure you take that with you, by the way; I don't want it."

"Yeah, I will." He stood in the doorway for a moment, looking uncomfortable. "I suppose I'd better be going."

"Okay."

"Thanks for, you know, bringing me back and cleaning me up and stuff." His eyes briefly flicked up to meet mine and then he quickly looked back down at his dirty sneakers.

"No problem," I laughed. "Don't worry about the clothes. They're all pretty old anyway, so keep anything you want and just dump the rest."

"You sure?"

"Yeah."

There were a few more moments of uncomfortable silence, and then he turned for the door. The trash bag was sitting there. "I'll be going then," he said, back over his shoulder.

"Bye, Marco. And the next time you drink yourself insensible, find somewhere safer than the park to do it."

It was after seven by the time I got home from work that Saturday evening. I grabbed a frozen dinner from the freezer and popped it into the microwave while I hastily jumped into the shower. Time was getting on and I had a hot date—with my Greek goddess, Sophia.

It seemed that it wasn't all over between us after all. I'd gotten a text message from her during the afternoon telling me that she was sorry; she said that she didn't believe any of that rubbish about me trying to get off with her mother. I wasn't impressed and decided to ignore it, but a short while later a second text arrived. In this one she said that she loved me and she thought we had something special together. *Yeah, right.* The third text begged me to contact her. By this stage I was starting to thaw and so I gave her a call. After just a few minutes of talking, it was like our fight had never happened. We arranged that I would pick her up after work and we'd go to a club, then later back to my place. I could hardly wait; the sex was always especially hot after we'd had a fight.

I knocked on their front door—they had the second-from-the-end unit in a townhouse—and it was answered a moment later by Helena, Sophia's mother. I immediately tensed right up.

"Hello, Edward." Helena gave me a warm and friendly smile—it reminded me of a crocodile I'd seen at the zoo. "Come on in. Sophia's upstairs; she'll be ready in a minute."

I warily followed her into the hallway. *Is she going to try something again?* Framed pictures hung against flowered wallpaper, which complimented the plush carpet. The décor was unmistakably feminine. *Not my taste at all.*

"Come right through," she said, heading into the living room.

"No, don't worry. I'll be fine here," I replied. Helena appeared all sweetness and light, but I couldn't forget what she'd tried to do to me the last time I was here. I would rather keep away from her as much as possible, at least until things settled down.

"Have it your way then." She gave me a rather simple shrug and then disappeared into the living room. I could hear the sounds of the television through the open doorway. I waited for several minutes, glancing occasionally at my watch. Even though I'd been late arriving, Sophia was still not ready. This wasn't exactly unexpected, since Sophia was never ready when she said she would be. There was the sound of rapid footsteps on the stairs and I glanced up.

Marco was on his way down, dressed in a pair of baggy jeans and a dark blue hoodie. He froze when he saw me in the hallway. "Edward?"

"Hi, Marco. How you feeling?"

He looked uncomfortable and quickly glanced back up the stairs to check that there was no sign of Sophia before looking back at me. "Please don't tell Sophia or Mum anything about last night," he begged, keeping his voice very soft.

"I won't say anything," I told him. The light in the hallway was quite dim, but as I looked at Marco I noticed a bruise under one of his eyes that hadn't been there earlier. "What happened to your face?" I asked, casually. "Have you been fighting again?"

He immediately looked away, turning his head so that the bruise wasn't visible. "I bumped it on a door," he said. "It's nothing."

He was obviously lying, but just as obviously didn't want to talk about it, so I didn't press him about it. Besides, at that moment, Sophia appeared at the top of the stairs, and she looked incredible. The skimpy pink top she was wearing left nothing to the imagination, and the tiny black skirt showed off every inch of her long, slim legs. "Wow!" It was all I could think of to say.

She grinned at me as she slowly made her way down the stairs. She obviously knew the effect she had on me, and she revelled in it. Almost at the bottom of the stairs, she stopped and turned her attention to her brother, who, like me, was staring at her. "What do you think you're looking at, perv," she said viciously. She gave a Marco a hard shove and, as he happened to be standing on the bottom step, he lost his balance, staggering until he managed to get his hand on the wall and catch himself.

He didn't say anything, but he shot his sister a look of pure hatred.

"Sophia, what did you do that for?" I demanded.

"He was in my way," she said, as if that were excuse enough. "Besides, I don't like him looking at me."

"You don't seem to mind anyone else looking at you," I pointed out.

"Yeah, but he's a dirty little pervert." Sophia's lip curled up in contempt as she sneered at her twin, then she turned her head back to look at me and was instantly all smiles. I found the sudden change creepy and a little scary. "Let's go," she said. "We're already late; you said you'd be here for eight."

I sighed, but didn't bother to waste my time pointing out that I'd been standing here in the hallway for ten minutes waiting for her to get ready. "See you around, Marco," I said to the boy, as Sophia dragged me out through the front door.

We got into my car and set off for the club. I have to admit that it did feel good to be back with Sophia. She was always hot, but tonight she was extra hot, and every guy in the club was going to be looking at her and wishing she was his and not mine.

"Is Marco alright?" I asked, as we drove along the street.

"What do you mean, is he alright?"

"Well, he sort of seems unhappy all the time. And then there's the bruises he's sporting."

"How should I know?" she demanded in a petulant tone of voice. "He probably got himself beaten up trying to pick up guys or something."

"Pick up guys?" I repeated in surprise. I looked at her.

"Oh yeah, my twin brother's a little gay-boy." She sounded rather gleeful telling me that. "Mom found some porno mags in his bedroom showing guys doing stuff together. Really disgusting stuff."

This came as a shock. My mind instantly went back to the previous night when I'd stripped him naked and stuck him under the shower, and then dried him off. *And then I'd shared my bed with him.* The thought made me a little uncomfortable. Though in spite of this, I still couldn't help being concerned about him. "Doesn't it bother you that he might be getting hurt?"

"Why should it bother me? He asks for it. He's always been weird. Anyway, what are you so worried about him for, Eddie? It's me that you should be concentrating on tonight."

"I know." I inhaled sharply as she slid her hand up my thigh, then down between my legs, squeezing my dick and balls through my pants. All thoughts of Marco vanished instantly. Tonight was going to be fucking amazing.

Chapter Three

I was awoken by the sound of the door bell.

I raised my head and blearily looked at the clock by the side of my bed. Ten o'clock. I pulled the duvet up around my head; it was far too early to face the world. Whoever it was could go to hell.

Last night had been totally wild. I'd been at the club with Sophia until around one thirty, and then we'd come back to my place. The sex had been even better than I had anticipated. We'd fucked each other like animals. I came twice and Sophia, well, from the noises she was making the whole session must have been one long orgasm for her.

By the time we were done we were both totally exhausted. I was ready for sleep, but Sophia insisted that I take her home. This was one of the strange things about her: all the time we've been together, she'd never once stayed over. We'd fought about it more than once. The last thing a guy wants after a heavy session is to have to get dressed and go for a drive. I'd thought—hoped—that last night might have been different, but no, she wanted to go home, and I'd long since learned that the easiest thing is always to give her what she wants. It had been some time after four a.m. when I'd finally crawled back into my bed, alone, to sleep. And now some inconsiderate bastard was trying to get me out of bed at the crack of dawn!

The door bell sounded again.

"Shit!" I threw back the duvet and stormed to the door, ready to give whoever it was hell. "Who is it?" I demanded, talking into the intercom system next to the door.

"It's me, Marco."

"Marco? What do you want?"

"I brought back the clothes you lent me."

"I told you not to bother; that you could keep them." I gave a sigh. "Oh, what the hell. I suppose you'd better come up." I pressed the button that released the lock on the front door of the building so he could come inside.

A few seconds later, Marco was at my door. As I let him in, he walked passed me and into the living room. He was carrying a black plastic bag.

"I told you I didn't want them back," I repeated, this time to his face. I must have looked annoyed, since he cringed back from me. I gave another sigh. "Look, I'm sorry. I'm feeling a bit cranky this morning because I didn't get much sleep. Thanks for bringing the stuff back."

Marco gave a sort of grin. "Yeah, you look a bit rough," he said, looking me up and down.

I was suddenly all too aware that I was standing there in just a pair of red silk boxers. Sophia's words from last night came back to me and I shuffled uncomfortably. I quickly told myself not to be so silly; even if Marco was gay, he was hardly likely to be interested in me. He was just a kid and I was a lot older. "I hope that's not the same bag you took your own stuff home in," I said, more to divert his attention from my exposed body than for any other reason.

"No. It's a different one. The clothes aren't washed though." He looked apologetic as he held out the bag towards me.

"Thanks. I suppose now that I'm up I may as well grab a shower and get myself dressed," I said. "Thanks again for bringing my things back." I moved back towards the door, to let him out.

"No problem. Hey, while you shower, why don't I fix you a coffee?" He turned and vanished into the kitchen.

"Marco, there's really no need..."

"You go ahead and get your shower. You take sugar?"

"Marco...no," I sighed. "No sugar." I gave up and left him in the kitchen while I went into the bathroom.

By the time I'd showered and cleaned myself up and pulled some fresh clothes on, I was starting to feel a little bit less grumpy and more tolerant. Being a day off, I dressed in some comfortable nylon track pants and a loose light green tee-shirt. Though as I entered the kitchen this tolerance was clearly about to be put to the test. There was the awful smell of burnt toast hanging heavy in the air. "Marco, what the hell are you doing?"

"I'm sorry. I was trying to make you breakfast and I forgot to watch the toast." The look on the boy's face was hard to describe; a kind of cross between panic and guilt. "You're not mad with me, are you?"

I stood and looked at him for a second, keeping my expression neutral, then I gave a grin; I couldn't possibly be angry with him when he looked like that. *Like a puppy dog.* "For goodness sake open the window and let some fresh air in. What on Earth possessed you to start messing about with breakfast? I thought you were only making coffee."

He pushed open the window and turned back to face me. "I sort of wanted to say thanks for what you did for me the other night, you know, fetching me back here and cleaning me up and stuff." His face reddened and he looked down at his feet. "And for not telling Mum or Sophia about it."

"Well, I could hardly leave you there in the park, could I?" I picked up the mug of coffee he'd prepared for me and took a drink. *Better than the toast at least.* That first shot of morning caffeine just tasted so good. "Aren't you having one?" I asked.

Marco shook his head. "Don't like it much."

"There's some juice in the fridge. Help yourself to some of that."

"Thanks." He quickly found a glass and poured himself some orange juice. He then sat down at the kitchen table while I leaned back against one of the counters.

"You look a bit healthier than last time you were here," I said.

He gave me a smile.

"Except for the new bruise on your face," I added and noticed that the smile instantly disappeared. I walked over and sat down at the table, opposite him. "Marco, you want to tell me where the bruises are coming from? Are you fighting with someone?"

Marco looked up at me, and for moment it seemed as though he was going to tell me what had been going on. But then he shook his head and lowered his eyes back down to his juice. "It's nothing," he said.

"Alright. As I said yesterday, it's none of my business. But you shouldn't let anyone use you as a punch-bag. Doesn't your mother ask you where the bruises come from?"

He turned his glass round in his fingers. "She doesn't care about me," he muttered. "She only cares about Sophia."

I gave a sympathetic smile. "I remember using a similar line with my own mother when I was about your age. I think it's a traditional thing for teenagers to feel like that about their parents."

Marco looked up at me and a spark of anger flashed in his eyes. "Don't talk to me like I'm a little kid!" he snarled. "I'm not a kid. You don't know what you're talking about."

"Sorry," I said, quickly, anxious to avoid the onset of a teenage tantrum.

He sat with a scowl on his face. "Everybody talks to me like I'm a kid." He took a drink of his juice and lowered the glass back to the table top. "I'm seventeen you know."

I tried not to laugh. He barely looked sixteen, sitting there in his oversized clothes, his long, untidy hair hanging down over his face. He bore an almost startling resemblance to Sophia which, rather unfortunately for him, tended to make him look pretty rather than handsome.

"The exact same day as Sophia's."

"She keeps reminding me that it's coming up," I said, with a smile.

"She's always been like that. It's all a big to-do. It's her big day and she likes to make sure that everyone else forgets all about me. She just wants to make sure that no one forgets to get her a present."

"It would be more than my life is worth."

"I sure won't be getting her anything," said Marco, bitterly.

"You don't like her very much, do you?"

"Not much, no." He took another drink of his juice, draining his glass.

I'd already finished my coffee so I stood up. "I suppose I'd better get something done," I said. "I'll let you out."

"You want me to go?"

"I thought you might have things to do."

"Not really. What are you doing today?"

"Sunday is my cleaning day," I told him. "Dusting, polishing, that sort of thing. I can't afford a maid just now, so I have to do it myself."

"I could stay and help," he suggested.

"You've got to be kidding me. Are you telling me you've nothing better to do that help me with my housework?"

He shook his head. "Please. I want to help."

Looking at those big round eyes in that innocent face, how could I possibly refuse? "Okay, if that's what you want."

We spent a good couple of hours on my weekly "mucking out", as I liked to call it. I'm not sure that Marco was really all that much help, as he didn't appear to have much idea when it came to cleaning, but having him around did make the time seem to go faster.

It was odd really. I'd never had much to do with him prior to this past couple of days, apart from a few quick words in passing as I'd picked Sophia up or dropped her off, and he'd always appeared to be rather shy and awkward. It was nice to see some of that shyness wearing off as the morning went on. As he relaxed, he became more chatty, and we talked as we worked. Though I did notice that most of the talking was about me. Marco wanted to know about my job, what sort of music I liked, what my favourite films were, all sorts of trivial things, but he was, for some reason extremely reluctant to give any information about himself. For example, when I asked him what sort of things he liked to do, all I got was a shrug and a simple "just stuff".

"I think that will do for now?" I said, eventually glancing at my watch. It was coming up to one o'clock. "Don't you need to get home for lunch or anything?"

Marco shook his head. "We don't usually have lunch."

"Ah, okay. Well, when I'm on my own I usually open a tin or get something out of the freezer, but if you like we can go out."

A wide and totally delighted grin appeared on his face. "You mean me and you?"

"There's only us here. Who did you think I meant?"

"I dunno." Then his grin faded and he looked uncomfortable. "I'll have to pass this time around, Edward. I don't have any money."

"That's alright. It's my treat. Call it a thanks for helping me out this morning."

"You sure?" The grin was back. In fact, he looked happier than I'd ever seen him.

"Hey, I'm only offering to buy you lunch, not take you on holiday or buy you a car or anything," I said, laughing. "Where did you want to go; a sit-down restaurant lunch, or Micky Dees?"

He hesitated for a moment. "Micky Dees. Unless you'd rather go to a restaurant."

"Micky Dees is fine," I said. Marco might be like his sister in looks, but he was nothing like her in personality. Sophia would never have bothered to ask what I would rather do. She'd have demanded the restaurant too.

We went down to Micky Dees in my car. This was something else that Marco was completely thrilled about. He'd never been inside it before and he sat back in the low passenger seat, an awed look on his face as he stroked the leather upholstery.

"You like it?" I asked.

"It's brilliant," he ginned. "I wish I had a car like this."

"Get yourself a good job and one day you might have," I told him. "Still, I do have to make sacrifices. Having an expensive car means that I don't have much left for non-essential luxuries, like food."

A sudden look of worry flashed across his face. "You don't have to buy me lunch," he said.

"Relax," I said, laughing at his expression. "I was just joking."

Micky Dees was pretty busy for a Sunday afternoon. I asked Marco what he wanted, and then sent him off to find us a table, while I fought my way to the counters. Marco had decided he wasn't very hungry and asked for just a cheeseburger and a small cola. I'd gotten the impression that this was more out of politeness than anything else and so I ordered him a double cheeseburger, with a large portion of fries and a large cola, then added an extra portion of fries to the list, just to make sure.

Marco had managed to grab a small, two-seater table and I took the seat opposite him and began unloading the food from the tray. "I got a few extras, just in case you changed your mind about being hungry," I explained as he eyed the loaded tray.

As things turned out, the extra portions had been a good idea. Marco ate as though he hadn't had a decent meal in days. As he ate, he opened up some more and now seemed almost completely at ease with me. For my part, I have to admit that I enjoyed his company; there was a sort of innocence, a lack of guile about him, that made him easy to spend time with. This was in Marcoed contrast with his sister. Sophia often left me wondering what was going on in her head, and I found myself having to watch what I said, just in case she took offence.

A short distance away from us was a rowdy group of guys who looked to be in their late teens. During our meal, I noticed Marco spending more and more time looking across at them, and at one of them in particular; a curly haired, blond boy, who looked like he'd spent half his life in the gym. There was no denying that this kid was good-looking, but boy did he know it; you could tell by the way he did everything he could to draw attention to himself. Marco realized I'd caught him staring at the guy, and quickly looked down at the remains of his food, his face colouring.

"Is that someone you know?" I asked.

Marco shook his head, keeping his eyes down.

I gave a short, soft laugh. "Maybe someone you'd like to get to know?"

At this, Marco did look up, his expression guarded. "What do you mean?" he asked, going onto the defensive.

"Don't worry," I grinned. "Sophia told me about the magazines; I know you like boys." *Whoops!* Even before I'd finished speaking, I knew I was saying exactly the wrong thing. But I couldn't stop myself. It was as though I was driving down a steep hill and my brakes weren't working.

The colour had drained from Marco's face and he stared at me, his eyes cold. Suddenly, he jumped to his feet, knocking over his paper cup of cola in the process, and headed for the door.

"Marco!" As he stormed past me, I made a grab for his arm and missed. "Marco, hold on." I struggled to get my legs out from under the table and hurried after him, aware that we were causing a scene and that all eyes in the place were on us. "Marco, just wait a minute," I shouted, as the door closed behind me. Marco was already striding away across the parking lot. I broke into a run and, catching up with him, I grabbed his elbow, bringing him to a halt and swinging him around to face me.

"She'd no right," he snapped. "She'd no right to tell you. She always has to try and spoil everything for me. She's an evil bitch."

"Hey, now hold on," I said, automatically coming to Sophia's defence, even though I knew that Marco was right, she could sometimes act a little thoughtlessly. "Just cool it a bit will you?"

"Why should I?"

"Well..." I tried to think of something to calm him down. "Because standing here in the car park, shouting, is not achieving anything except to put on a show for that lot." I nodded back towards the restaurant, where several interested faces could be seen watching us through the large glass windows.

"I don't care," he said, much quieter.

"Why is it such a big deal that she told me about you anyway?"

"Because she's trying to turn you against me, just like she turns everyone against me, just like she's done all the way through school. I have no friends. Everyone thinks I'm weird because of her. Everybody likes pretty Sophia, and I'm just her weirdo twin brother who everybody laughs at."

"I'm not laughing at you," I pointed out. "And it doesn't matter to me that you're gay. I have friends who are gay."

"Yeah, sure," he said bitterly.

"Look, get in the car and I'll take you back to my place and we can talk properly, instead of discussing things here in public."

"I don't want to," said Marco, petulantly.

"Oh, well, if you want to act like a little kid, fine. But I'm going. You can walk home."

"Fine."

He turned away and started walking towards the main road.

I went to my car and got in. *Shit*! I banged my hands down on the steering wheel. I'd handled that pretty badly. One minute we'd been getting on great, and the next we were brawling in public and I wasn't even sure exactly how it had come about. In a way, I could understand how Marco felt about Sophia; she can be pretty vindictive when she puts her mind to it. It must have been really tough growing up with a sister like that. Also, I had to admit that I liked Marco; he was a good kid, and I really didn't want to part with him like this. *Another one of your relationships crashes and burns*, a perverse little imp whispered in my thoughts. With a sigh, I started up the engine.

Marco hadn't got very far down the street.

I pulled up alongside him and hit the switch for the power window. "Marco?" He deliberately ignored me and continued walking. "Come on, Marco, get in," I said.

He glanced over at me and shook his head. "You only want me to get in because you feel sorry for me."

I realized that this was partly true. "Yes, I feel a bit sorry for you," I admitted. "But I like you as well. I don't know what we're fighting about. It was Sophia who gave your secret away, so why fight with me about it?"

He stopped, causing me to have to brake. Luckily there was no one following behind me. "Because she's not here and you are," he said. There was a slight flicker at the corner of his mouth as if he were starting to realise just how silly this all was.

"Come on, get it," I said, leaning over to open the door for him.

He hesitated a moment and then climbed into the passenger seat. "I'm only getting in because I want to have another ride in this cool car," he said.

"Sure thing," I grinned.

Trying to look as though he were doing it purely for my benefit, Marco got into the car. He sat there with frown on his face.

"So, where do you want to go?" I asked.

He shrugged. "Home, I suppose."

"Yours or mine?"

He was silent for a moment then raised his eyes to look at me. He looked sad. "Mine," he said.

"No problem," I said, as we set off down the road. "Look, Marco, I meant what I said; it doesn't bother me in the slightest that you're gay."

He glanced up at me but then returned his gaze to the road ahead. He didn't speak.

I tried to think of something else to say but his cold silence made it difficult.

"You can drop me here," he said, as we approached the end of his street.

"I may as well take you to the house; we're nearly there anyway."

"No, I don't want you to," he said quickly. Then he slowly turned his head to look at me. "I don't want Sophia to know I've been with you," he explained.

"Okay, if that's what you want," I said, pulling up to the curb.

As the car came to a halt, Marco opened the door and put one foot out, but then he paused. Again he made eye contact with me. "I'm sorry about blowing up at you earlier," he said. "Thanks for taking me to Micky Dees."

"Hey, it was nothing," I said. "Thanks for helping me with the cleaning and stuff. And don't worry, I won't say anything about this morning to Sophia. It can be our secret."

"Thanks," he smiled, shyly. He got out of the car, but then bent and put his head back inside the door. He looked at me, uncertainly. "Edward, would it be okay if I came around to your place sometimes? I won't get in the way, I swear. And I sure won't come whenever Sophia's there."

The request took me by surprise. What could I say? An open refusal would probably upset him, and I really didn't want to do that. Besides, up until the minor eruption after lunch, today had been sort of fun. "I guess that would be okay," I said.

"Thanks," he grinned. "I'll see you around."

"Yeah, take care, Marco. I'll see you around," I replied.

The boy seemed to have a spring in his step as he strode towards his front door.

Chapter Four

I know that most people don't like Mondays, but strangely enough I've never minded them. Then again, I've never really been one to follow the crowds. And this particular Monday I had an extra reason to be happy: tonight I had another date with Sophia. I usually didn't see much of her during the week seeing as she was at college and her mother didn't approve of her being out on a "school night". So we'd made a compromise that I could see her on a couple of nights during the week as long as I didn't keep her out too late, and then we could make up for that on Fridays and Saturdays.

Happily anticipating an evening of fun, I left work at around four-thirty, and even the sudden torrential shower as I drove home did nothing to dampen my mood. I had to drive past the front door of the apartments in order to reach the private parking lot at the rear, and as I did so I noticed a sorry-looking figure huddled in the doorway, trying unsuccessfully to shelter from the pouring rain. Marco.

Quickly, I parked the car in my allotted space, entered the apartment building through the back door, and hurried straight through to the front to open the door for the sodden boy. "Marco, what're you doing standing there in the rain? It's pissing down."

"I was waiting for you. You said it would be alright to come round sometimes," he replied, shaking his long, wet hair back from his eyes.

"Yeah, but you were only here yesterday," I said. How would he have known what time I got off work? How long was he going to stand there waiting for me? "And I've got a date with Sophia later."

"You don't want me to stay?" he asked, looking hurt. "I'm sorry. I'll go then."

"Don't be silly," I said, quickly. "You'd better come in; at least until the rain stops. I just didn't expect to see you today, that's all." I led him up the stairs and into my apartment, where he stood in the hallway, miserably dripping onto the carpet.

Looking at him, I found it impossible to stop myself from grinning. "You can't just stand around like that," I said. "There's a clean towel in the bathroom, so go and get out of those wet clothes and bring them through to the kitchen and I'll toss them into the dryer for you."

As Marco disappeared into the bathroom, the front door buzzer sounded.

Now what? I pressed the intercom button. "Hello?"

"Hello sexy," came a familiar, effeminate, but most definitely male voice. "Are you ready to let me run my fingers through your hair?"

"Oh, hi, Angel. Come on up." I pressed the door release. I'd completely forgotten that I'd arranged to have my hair cut this evening. *The perils of a hectic social schedule,* I thought in amusement. *I might have to start using a date planner.*

'Angel Kristophos' ran a mobile hairdressing business. I had him call round once a month to keep me looking tidy. Angel, or rather Angelo, as he was really called, was the younger brother of one of my old school friends, and so I'd known him for years. He had always been a little on the effeminate side, but since he'd left school and gone into hairdressing, his gay manner was now so extreme that it was almost a caricature. I was sure much of it was an act, put on to fit in with the stereotypical image of the gay hairdresser. Angelo, however, was always amusing to be around. He had personality to spare and he flirted with absolutely everybody, though it was all in harmless fun, or at least I hoped it was.

"I'd forgotten you were coming by tonight," I explained as I let Angelo into the apartment and led him through to the kitchen.

Angelo was a swarthy Greek, with black curly hair and olive skin. He walked passed me and dropped his bag down on the kitchen table before putting his hands on his hips and looking offended. "You'd forgotten?" He allowed his voice to climb into a falsetto. "How could you possibly forget about arranging for me to come over here and work my exclusive magic upon you?" His hands were waving about wildly as he talked.

How indeed? "I've sort of got other things on my mind," I explained.

"So I see," said Angelo, his eyes widening as he stared past me. "Well hel-lo sweetie."

I turned quickly to find Marco standing there wearing nothing but a brown towel, which he held in place with one hand whilst clutching a pile of wet clothes in the other. He had a surprised look on his face. "Sorry," he muttered, as he hurriedly handed me his clothes and, red-faced, fled back towards the bathroom.

Angelo had turned towards me. He stood with his arms folded in front of him, one eyebrow raised questioningly.

"Don't look at me like that," I said, feeling that I'd been caught out in some sort of indiscretion, even though the whole situation was totally innocent. "He's just a friend."

"Obviously a very close one," said Angelo, the corner of his mouth twitching.

"It's nothing like that," I said, defensively.

"Like what?"

"Like what you mean."

"Oh don't worry about that, darling," said Angelo giving me another wave. "Your little secret's completely safe with me. You can go right on pretending that you're straight."

"But I am straight."

Angelo ignored me and began getting his bits and pieces out of his bag. "I always knew you were really one for the boys; I'm never wrong about these things. He's very sweet, but he needs a bit more meat on his bones, and he is bit young. How old is he, thirteen? Where did you find him?"

"He's seventeen! He's my girlfriend's twin brother."

"Your girlfriend's brother? What perfect camouflage, you sly dog you."

"Oh, I give up," I said, exasperated.

Angelo gave a soft giggle as he watched me put Marco's clothes into the dryer. "If you're even doing his laundry for him, it must be true love."

"It's pouring outside, just in case you hadn't noticed. That's why he's dressed in a towel. His clothes got wet while he was waiting for me to come home and I'm drying them off for him."

"If you say so."

While Angelo finished getting himself ready, I went through into my bedroom and pulled out a clean pair of shorts and a shirt for Marco to wear until his own stuff was dry. It wouldn't do for him to be wandering around in just a towel, especially while Angelo was here. I opened the bathroom door to find Marco totally naked, the towel wrapped around his head as he used it to dry his hair.

"Oops, sorry," I said. "I should have knocked first."

Marco automatically moved his hands to cover himself, but then he smiled shyly and resumed his towelling. "That's okay," he said. "You've already seen everything."

I didn't reply.

"I didn't realize there was anyone else there or I wouldn't have come out like that."

"Don't worry about it, it's only Angelo," I explained, running my eyes up and down the boy's naked body. "He's come to cut my hair. Here, you can put these on while you wait for your own things to dry." I handed him the shirt and shorts.

Back in the kitchen, Angelo was now ready for me. I sat down and let him get on with it, closing my eyes and letting my mind drift. As far as Angelo was concerned, it wasn't necessary to try to make conversation, since he was capable of doing that all on his own. He talked incessantly, giving me all the latest gossip: who was dating who, or who was cheating on who. I knew some of the people he was talking about, but most of the names were ones I'd never heard of, and I wasn't especially interested in any of it, so I just let him chatter away in the background. The monthly "tidy up" didn't take long, and when Angelo announced that he had finished, I opened my eyes to find Marco sitting up on the worktop, watching.

"So, what do you think?" Angelo asked Marco.

Marco gave a shrug. "He looks okay, but he always looks like that; it's not really much different from when you started."

"Not much different. Not much different?" said Angelo, the pitch of his voice rising as he took offence at the reMarco. "I'll have you know, boy, that I'm an *artiste*. Not that you would appreciate that, given the state of your untidy mop." He flicked his fingers through the ends of Marco's long hair. Then he turned back to me. "Would you like me to attempt to tidy up your number-one boy while I'm here?"

"Marco is a friend, he's not my 'boy,'" I protested. "He probably could do with a bit of a tidy up, but that's up to him."

"How about it?" said Angelo, taking hold of Marco's chin and frowning as he moved the boy's head from side to side. "You've got a really sweet face. Put yourself in my hands and I could make you look stunning."

"Erm, I dunno," said Marco, shooting me a worried look.

"It's up to you," I said. "Don't let him bully you into it if you don't want it cutting. Angelo is pretty good though."

"I am superb," Angelo informed us.

"I...I don't have any money," Marco stammered, looking uncomfortable.

Angelo gave him a grin. "Edward will pay; he's loaded."

"Not exactly loaded," I quickly pointed out. "But I think I can afford to pay for a haircut. Go ahead, Marco. I'll take care of it."

Marco and I swapped places and it was my turn to sit and watch as Angelo went to work. It took him much longer to tidy up Marco's unkempt locks than it had taken to trim mine, but when he'd done, the transformation was incredible. I had to admit that Marco did look good: short at the sides and gelled and slightly spiky at the front, the style really suited him.

Angelo held up a mirror and Marco stared worriedly into it, as if unsure whether he liked this new look. He glanced up at me for reassurance.

"You look great," I said.

Instantly his face lit up with a smile. "Yeah, I guess it does look pretty cool."

By this stage, Marco's clothes were dry, and he went into the bathroom to get changed while I let Angelo out.

"He's really sweet," Angelo told me. "And he all but worships the ground you walk on."

"What are you talking about?" I asked, a little shocked at the comment.

"Don't tell me you haven't noticed," laughed Angelo. "He never takes his eyes off you. Can't say that I blame him either."

"You're letting your imagination run away with you again," I told him. "There's nothing like that going on. We're just friends, nothing else."

"Have it your own way," he said with a knowing look. "But I'm telling you, in his head you are much more than friends. By the way, what's with all the bruises on his chest and face? Looks like somebody has been playing rough with him."

"I don't know. I think something's going on, but he won't talk about it."

"Oh well, I suppose we all have our little secrets, don't we?" He patted my cheek. "See you next month, and be a good boy until then."

"Yeah. Bye, Angelo."

I closed the door and turned to find Marco coming out of the bathroom, now dressed in his own dry clothes. He smiled at me, almost shyly, and I couldn't help thinking about Angelo's words. *Could Marco have a crush on me?* No, that was just stupid. *We were just friends; Marco knew that.*

"Thanks for paying for the haircut, Edward," said the teen. "It's going to take some getting used to. I do like it though."

"It looks really good," I agreed. "You shouldn't have any trouble finding yourself a boyfriend now."

"You think?" He stood looking at me, thoughtfully, his bottom lip held lightly between his teeth.

I sighed inwardly. "Marco, you know...well...you understand that I'm going out with your sister. I do like you and everything, you're a great kid, but I'm not...well, I'm not gay."

Marco's face flushed and he looked away. Could there have been a trace of disappointment there, or was it just Angelo's wild ideas stimulating my over-active imagination? I hoped that I hadn't hurt the boy too much, and I was already wishing that I'd kept my mouth shut. After a moment, Marco raised his head, a worried look in his eyes. "We can still be friends though, can't we?"

"Of course we can," I reassured him.

He brightened instantly and gave an impish grin. "And I can still be your number-one boy?"

"Number-one boy?"

"It's what Angelo called me."

I sighed again, this time aloud. *Angelo has a lot to answer for.*

I prepared a quick snack for myself and Marco and left the boy playing a game on my Xbox while I got changed and ready for my date with Sophia. I selected a nice wine-coloured silk shirt and dark slacks which clung to my legs in a rather nice fashion.

"You look good," Marco said with a smile, looking up as I entered the living room.

"Thanks. You think Sophia will be impressed?"

The smile immediately disappeared. "She probably won't even notice," he said, a trace of bitterness in his voice. "Sophia's not bothered about what you look like, just as long as she's getting what she wants. I don't know why you bother with her."

"Marco!" I said, a hint of warning in my voice.

Scowling, the boy turned his attention back to his game.

The rain had eased off to just a light drizzle by the time I was ready to go, and Marco insisted that I drop him off at the end of his street, saying that he would walk the rest of the way. I pointed out that this was silly since I was obviously going all the way to his house, but he was adamant about it, muttering something about not wanting Sophia to find out that he'd been with me. So I gave in and let him have his own way.

Amazingly enough, Sophia was almost ready for me; she was on her way down the stairs as her mother opened the door to let me into the hallway. And she looked stunning as ever. As she reached the bottom of the stairs I put my arms around her neck and kissed her lips.

"You look incredible," I murmured, nuzzling her neck.

She giggled, girlishly.

At that moment, Marco arrived home, letting himself him. He froze for a second, a slight grimace crossing his face as he took in the sight of Sophia and me holding each other.

As he squeezed past us to get to the stairs, Sophia caught his shoulder, turning him around to face her. "What do you think you look like?" the girl snorted, her eyes on his hair. She gave a derisive laugh and put out her hand and squashed down the short, gelled spikes above his forehead.

"Get off me!" Marco snarled, batting her hand away.

"You look stupid," Sophia laughed.

"What would you know?" Marco demanded, looking hurt.

Her hand was once more reaching for his head and he roughly pushed it away.

"Sophia, leave him alone," I said, grabbing her arm myself and pulling it to me. "I think he looks really good. It suits him."

Marco shot me a grateful glance, but Sophia turned back to me, shaking her head.

"As if you'd know," said the girl. "You've got no taste at all."

"How can you say I've no taste?" I grinned. "I picked you, didn't I?"

"That's different," she replied. "Besides, it was me who picked you."

Anything I might have said in answer to that was cut off as her lips once again pressed against mine. Over her shoulder, I watched Marco give us a cold look and then he turned and headed off up the stairs.

Chapter Five

When I'd told Marco that it would be okay for him to call round sometimes, I hadn't expected him to visit my apartment every single day. However, that's exactly what happened.

Every day, I would arrive home from work to find him waiting on my doorstep. His eagerness to spend time with me was a little disturbing, and there was always that nagging memory of Angelo's suggestion that Marco had a crush on me. A couple of times, I almost suggested to him that maybe it would be better if he didn't come round quite so often, but when it came down to it, I couldn't bring myself to say anything that might upset him. Besides, if I were being honest with myself, I liked having him around.

We'd just talk, for the most part, and he'd tell me about his day at school and then listen attentively while I told him about anything that had happened to me at work. If I'd had a bad day, he would listen sympathetically and then make some joke which would immediately lighten my mood. If I wasn't in the mood to talk or there was anything that I needed to get on with, he'd sit quietly at the kitchen table doing some school-work. Then I'd prepare something to eat and we'd eat together; he always ate as though he were ravenous and I was constantly amazed that anyone with such a slight build could put away so much food. On one occasion I joked about him not being fed at home, and he immediately looked uncomfortable. It was obvious that Marco wasn't happy at home; I knew he didn't get on with Sophia, but it seemed to go far deeper than that. However, any time I tried to bring up the subject of his home life, he instantly clammed up and made it clear that he didn't want to discuss it. Most evenings I'd drive him home, and he always insisted that I drop him off at the end of Grove Street in order that his mother and sister didn't find out that he'd been with me. He also begged me not to tell Sophia anything about his visits to my apartment. I couldn't see the reason for all of this secrecy, but if that's what he wanted, I didn't see any harm in going along with it.

On Friday evening, Marco was there on the doorstep, waiting for me, as usual. I reminded him that I had a date with Sophia tonight, so this would have to be a short visit. He gave me a disappointed frown and I responded with a warning look.

"Sorry," Marco muttered. He didn't look sorry, but he did look chastened, and he let the subject drop. Every time Sophia's name was mentioned there was the same unmistakable tension in the air. Marco's dislike of his sister caused him to make frequent derogatory comments about her, and he had even hinted on several occasions that she didn't feel anything for me. He claimed that she would lose interest in me as soon as a better prospect came along. But even though I couldn't deny the truth of some of the things he said about her, she was still my girlfriend, and I always rose automatically to her defence.

I closed the door behind us and kicked off my shoes. "I'm going to go and have a hot shower," I told him. "You'll have to amuse yourself for a while."

"Fine." Marc shrugged. "I'll go watch some TV." He shrugged and wandered into the living room.

I left him to it and went into my bedroom where I quickly stripped off my polo shirt and slacks and, wrapping a towel around my waist, I headed for the bathroom. I was really looking forward to tonight. Since it was the weekend it meant that there was no curfew, and so I didn't have to take Sophia back home early. The two of us were going out to a club, and then it would be back to my apartment for some hot sex. I hadn't seen Sophia since the previous Monday, and we hadn't had sex since Saturday. A quick wank is fine, but it doesn't compare with the real thing. I felt my cock start to harden as I imagined us on my bed, screwing the night away. Tonight was going to be so good.

The hot shower felt great: really relaxing after a hard day. I soaped the front of my body, paying particular attention to my groin and, in the process, stroking myself to a full erection. Pulling my hand away from my rock-hard, twitching cock took a big effort; I knew that if I were to jack off now, it wouldn't be quite so good later, so I was determined to save myself. Forcing myself to ignore my aching boner, I reached for the shampoo, massaging it into my hair to form a rich, soapy lather, and then dipping my head under the spray to rinse it away.

"Edward...?"

"Marco? What do you want?" I demanded, trying to open my eyes and, of course, I got soap in them.

Marco was standing in the bathroom doorway, his eyes wide as he stared at me.

I suddenly realized that he was staring at my exposed erection, and I quickly put my hand down to cover myself. "What did you want, Marco?" I asked again.

"Oh, yeah," he shook himself and he grinned at me shyly. "Your cell-phone's ringing. I thought you might want to know."

I listened carefully and, over the splash of the water from the shower, I could just make out the trilling ring of my cell-phone. "Oh, erm, thanks. Go get it for me, will you?"

As Marco went to fetch me the phone, I hurriedly rinsed the soap from my eyes and reached for a towel. The call probably wouldn't be important and I would be able to ring them back later anyway, but sending Marco for the phone meant that I could get rid of him for long enough to cover myself up. I wasn't normally all that inhibited when it comes to my body, but given my suspicions about the way Marco felt about me, standing in front of him with a raging boner was perhaps not such a good idea. The ringing had in fact stopped by the time Marco returned. Holding the dark green towel in place with one hand, I accepted the phone from him, thumbing the buttons to find out who had been calling. It had been Sophia. I immediately pressed a button to call her back. *Gotta love that speed dial.*

"Hiya gorgeous. What's up?" I said into the phone, ignoring the disapproving scowl on Marco's face.

"*Hi, Ed,*" Sophia responded. She was using her "sweet little girl" voice.

I was immediately on guard as this could only mean that she wanted something.

"*About tonight...something's come up,*" she told me.

"What came up?"

"*Danica just broke up with that swine of a boyfriend she had. She's completely brokenhearted right now.*"

"I can imagine."

"*Megan, Cindy, Dot and I are getting together with her tonight. We simply have to take her out and cheer her up.*"

"I've had a rough week too, you know. I could probably do with some cheering up."

"*You'll be fine. This is a crisis.*"

"It's just a silly fight."

"*It is not.*"

"You didn't worry when you and I had that fight a few weeks back."

"*Of course I did. And they were all there for me, so I have to be there for them.*"

"But we had plans."

"*Oh, don't be so selfish! Look, Eddie, I'm already late. I'll see you tomorrow.*"

"Sophia!" I stared at the phone in my hand. "She cancelled on me," I said in a mixture of anger and disappointment.

Marco looked at me, and I half hoped that he might gloat at the situation so as to give me an excuse to lash out at someone, but he simply shook his head sadly and took back the phone as I held it out to him. He left me alone and, resignedly, I began to towel myself dry.

By the time I'd dried myself off and pulled on some jeans and a tee-shirt, I had decided that I may as well make the best of the situation.

"Well, Marco, it looks like we're both at loose ends for tonight. How about we go and rent a movie, get ourselves some take-out, and spend the evening in front of the TV?"

"That sounds like a great idea!" Marco, of course, was delighted with the idea.

The sudden change to my plans for the evening had been disappointing, especially as it meant that I'd now have to wait another day before indulging in the sexual frenzy which I had so eagerly been anticipating. However, sex aside, a "guys' night in" with Marco wasn't really such a bad substitute. Marco didn't require the constant attention and flattery that Sophia always demanded: Sophia had to be the centre of attention, whereas Marco was much more easy-going. And with Marco, I didn't have to watch what I said all the time. In fact, I realized, in a lot of ways I much preferred the boy's company to his sister's.

It was just a shame that Marco wasn't a girl.

Not that Marco and I agreed on everything, of course. In the rental store, we argued about what sort of movie to rent; I wanted an action movie, he wanted some sort of psychological horror thing. We compromised by getting one of each. Then, when it came to the take-out, I wanted Indian, while he wanted a pizza. In the end we both settled on Chinese. I discovered that even disagreeing with Marco was fun; our arguments were really just light-hearted banter, far removed from the tense, fiery fights that I constantly seemed to be involved in with Sophia.

Back at the apartment, I took two cans of beer from the fridge, found us some forks, pulled the curtains, and we sat down together on the couch to watch the first of the movies, eating the take-out directly from the foil cartons. The action movie was pretty bad, but we stuck it out to the bitter end, giving numerous groans and giggles along the way. As the final credits rolled, Marco couldn't resist a dig about how bad my choice had been.

"Alright, so I have shit taste in movies," I laughed. "I bet yours isn't much better."

"I bet it is."

"Bet it isn't."

He elbowed me playfully in the ribs and I gave him a push in return, sending him sprawling onto his side, laughing.

"You take this stuff into the kitchen, out of the way," I said indicating the piled up foil cartons, which were all that remained of our meal. "I'll swap the movies over."

Still laughing, Marco gathered up the trash and headed for the kitchen.

"Bring a couple more cans back with you," I called after him, and then bent down to change the disks in the DVD player.

I felt strangely happy. It couldn't be the effects of the alcohol, I thought, since we'd only had one can each. And it could hardly have been the crap movie.

"What's the matter?" Marco asked, grinning, as he came back from the kitchen.

"What do you mean?"

"You're looking at me funny."

"Well, you are sort of strange-looking," I replied.

Marco contorted his face into a weird expression, crossing his eyes, but could only hold it for a second before he burst out laughing again. He handed me one of the cans and we settled down to watch the second movie. This second movie was bloody scary. Okay, so I'm a wimp when it comes to anything like that, and I'm not ashamed to admit it.

Though in this case it looked like Marco was almost as scared as me. He was sitting pulled in on himself, one hand up to his mouth as he nervously chewed on the side of one of his fingers. The side of his leg was pressed up against my own and he was leaning towards me as if seeking the security of physical contact with someone else. I resisted a sudden, irrational urge to put my arm around his shoulders. On the screen a teenaged girl was wandering around inside a dark house—why do they always do that? I mean, two of her friends had already been horribly murdered by some insane, knife-wielding maniac in that very same house, and there she was wandering around in the dark. What sane person would do a thing like that? I wanted to scream "For God's sake, you stupid bitch, get the hell out of there!", but instead I watched in silence, my heart pounding and my nerves at breaking point. The girl entered another room and her hand fumbled for the light switch - at last she was doing something sensible, she was going to turn on the light. Suddenly a hand flew out, bony fingers wrapping vice-like around her wrist. She screamed.

I gave a scream of my own and almost pissed myself as a hand clamped down hard on my thigh. "Marco! What the hell...? You scared the shit out of me," I breathed. I put my hand to my chest to ensure that my heart hadn't packed up from the shock.

Marco was giggling almost hysterically. He let go of my thigh, his hand going to his mouth to try to hide his laughter. "Sorry," he managed to get out. "That was so funny."

"I'll show you funny," I replied, throwing myself on top of him. Marco gave a squeal and struggled to escape, but I was bigger and stronger than he was. As we wrestled, he managed to roll from the couch to the floor, but, before he could get up, I was on him again. His arms went around my neck, squeezing, but his grip loosened as my hand found his ribs and I began tickling him. We were both laughing and panting from our exertions. Eventually I managed to get a hold of his wrists and I pressed them to the floor above his head. He was flat on his back and I was lying full length on top of him. Our faces were just inches apart.

As we looked into each other's eyes, the laughter suddenly died away.

Marco licked his lips, his tongue flicking out nervously. I looked down at him. He was so like Sophia, yet at the same time he was so different. When I looked into Sophia's eyes I was always left wondering what was going on in her head. With Marco there was nothing hidden, and what I saw there scared me. Marco's breathing was slow and ragged. He licked his lips again and raised his head towards my own. I lowered my own head towards him.

What the hell was I doing?

I pulled back in horror and forced myself to my feet and turned away. I was about to kiss a seventeen-year-old boy. What the hell was the matter with me? Was I really so horny that I'd stoop to something like that?

"Edward?" Marco had also got to his feet and was standing behind me. He voice sounded small and frightened.

I turned back to face him, trying to get myself under control. "I think I'd better take you home," I said, forcing a smile.

"But…"

"It is getting late," I interrupted him. "And I'm feeling tired, and I do have to work tomorrow."

"I could stay here tonight," Marco suggested.

"Maybe not such a good idea," I said. "Let's get you home."

I lay there for hours, unable to sleep, turning onto one side and then onto the other in an effort to get comfortable. Even though it wasn't an especially warm night, I found myself sweating and I occasionally wafted the sheets to try to get some air to my body. Irritably, I thumped my pillow, trying to pound it into a shape that would give me more support and let me sleep. But unfortunately it wasn't the pillow that was the problem.

Each time I closed my eyes I could see Marco's face, looking at me, hurt in his eyes. The boy hadn't said a word all the way home. We'd travelled in silence, and after our earlier light-hearted banter, this lack of communication felt unnatural, uncomfortable, even oppressive. Marco didn't even speak to tell me to drop him at the end of the street, and so I took him all the way up to his gate. Wordlessly, he climbed out of the car. Just before he closed the door he looked back inside. "I'm sorry, Edward," he said, the words hardly audible. Then he was gone.

"Marco..." I'd called after him, but then realized that I'd purposely spoken too softly for him to hear. I'd sat and watched his silhouette walk up the path and disappear into his house before pulling away and driving home.

I was angry.

I was angry with Sophia for cancelling our date; if it hadn't been for her I wouldn't have spent the evening with Marco.

I was angry with Marco for his apparent dependence on me; he seemed to be there every time I turned around.

But most of all, I was angry with myself.

Angelo had warned me that Marco had a crush on me, and I'd not done anything about it. Why had I let Marco continue to come round every day? Was it vanity? Did I feel flattered because he had these feelings for me? No, I knew it wasn't anything like that. I let him keep coming round because I cared about him. He was a lonely kid who had needed someone, and that someone had turned out to be me. Besides, that was not the issue. The problem wasn't Marco's feelings for me—it was my feelings for Marco. Tonight I'd almost kissed him. How perverted was that? I'd been about to kiss a seventeen-year-old boy. My girlfriend's twin brother! I made up my mind there and then that things could not go on as they were. I'd have to talk to Marco and tell him that he couldn't come round so often. In fact, it would probably be best if he stayed away altogether. Marco wouldn't like it, of course, but he'd have to get used to the idea. His infatuation with me wasn't healthy, and my own feelings towards him were even worse.

My mind made up, I felt a little better, and I slowly drifted off into an uneasy sleep.

Sophia lay looking at me, her face just inches away from my own. The corners of her mouth twitched in what could have been a smile, but could just have easily have been a sneer. "So, are we going to fuck?" she asked. "Or do you prefer boys now?"

When I didn't answer, she flipped the duvet back from the bed leaving us both naked. She ran her hands down over her body, her mouth open and her tongue running over her lips. "You want this, Ed? Come on, fuck me."

I tried to answer her, but though my lips were moving, no sound would come out. I tried to reach for her, but my arms wouldn't move.

"Not much of a man, are you, Ed?" she sneered. Her painted fingernails were like red daggers and she ran one of them down my chest, and down over my stomach, then drew it slowly along my limp cock. I willed myself to respond, feeling that I should become aroused by her touch, wanting to become aroused, but nothing was happening.

"I always knew you were worthless, Ed," she said, coldly. Then her face softened. The hardness around her mouth gradually disappeared. Her expression became caring. And it wasn't Sophia there anymore, it was Marco. I let my eyes travel down his naked body, seeing how Sophia's soft curves had been replaced by Marco's thin, almost angular form.

"I love you, Edward," the boy said.

"No," I replied, finding my voice at last. "No, you can't."

"I do. I love you much more than Sophia ever will."

"It's no good, Marco. I'm not gay. I love Sophia."

"You don't really," he said. "You keep telling yourself that you love Sophia, but really you love me." His hand was on my chest, travelling down my body, following the same path that Sophia's fingers had taken just moments earlier. Then his fingers were around my cock and I was hardening under his touch. "You see, Edward," he smiled. "I told you it was me that you loved." He bent and took my swollen cock into his mouth.

"Don't, Marco," I begged. But I did nothing to stop him.

Then everything changed. One moment I'd been lying on my back, the next I was on my knees, even though I hadn't moved. Marco was on all fours in front of me. He raised his head and looked around at me, a grin on his face. "Do it," he said.

I knew what he meant, what he wanted. Slowly I pushed forwards, my erection sliding smoothly into his ass. As I entered him, a soft sigh escaped his lips. "I love you, Edward," he gasped.

"I'm only doing this because you asked me too," I told him. "I'm not gay. I love Sophia."

"If you say so, Edward," he smiled.

I thrust forwards, feeling the tightness of his hole around my cock. It was wonderful. I pulled back and thrust forwards again. Again. Again. It felt good. "I'm not gay," I said, between clenched teeth. "I'm not gay," I repeated with each thrust. "I'm not gay," I moaned, even as my whole body shook in the throes of orgasm.

Marco again turned to look at me, the soft smile still on his face.

Unwillingly I bent forwards towards him and we kissed lightly, our lips touching.

"If you say so," he said.

Chapter Six

I awoke with a start. I was covered with sweat. As I rolled onto my back I felt something wet against one of my legs. With a groan of self-disgust, I realized just what had happened. I climbed out of bed and pulled back the sheets to reveal a wet patch in the vicinity of where my groin had been. I'd had what was commonly referred to as a wet dream. I'd thought this was something that only happened to sex-starved, pubescent teenagers. *What the hell was happening to me?*

The clock on my bedside table said it was just after 6.00 a.m. A bit early for getting up on a Saturday morning, but I didn't feel like trying to sleep again, and besides, these sheets needed taking off. I usually wore my boxer shorts to bed, which would have limited the damage, but last night I'd been so warm and uncomfortable that I'd kicked them off and slept naked.

Still naked, I bundled up the sheets and padded through to the hallway closet where I pushed them into the washing machine and set it going. Then, bedclothes taken care of, it was time for a bit of personal cleansing. In the bathroom, I turned on the cold water tap and stepped under the shower, gasping as the icy water splashed down over my body. I forced myself to stand under the water for several minutes as if to try and wash away my guilty feelings, then gave in and turned on the hot tap. I gave myself a quick, but thorough soaping, and rinsed off before wrapping a towel around my waist and going in search of a strong cup of coffee.

As I sat drinking the coffee, I deliberately avoided thinking about my dream, hoping that it would quickly fade into a fuzzy haziness, as was usually the case with dreams. However, there was no avoiding the fact that I was going to have to do something about Marco. No doubt the boy would be round later, and I was going to have to break the bad news to him. I certainly wasn't looking forward to it.

There was no sign of Marco that morning. After I'd had some lunch, I went to work, partly relieved that the boy hadn't appeared, but at the same time feeling a little disappointed and even a little hurt. I wondered if maybe Marco had decided that since I wasn't going to let anything happen between us, it wasn't worth his time coming round anymore. Oh well, if that's all our friendship means to him then perhaps it is better if he does stay away. Work was unusually hectic, which was a blessing, as it kept my mind off my personal life.

Though amidst the hustle and bustle, I did find time to give Sophia a quick call and confirm that we were still on for tonight.

It was just past eight when I pulled up to the house to collect Sophia. She looked, if anything, even more stunning than usual, and the top she was wearing left nothing at all to the imagination. Just the sight of her dispelled any lingering doubts I might have had about my sexuality.

"Close your mouth, you're drooling," she giggled. She knew the effect she had on me. She had the same effect on almost every guy who saw her, and she always took full advantage of it.

"I hope I'm going to get to sample these goods you've got on display," I told her, softly, as I nuzzled at her ear and inhaled her perfume. It was one of the expensive brands that I had bought for her.

"That depends whether you're a good boy," she laughed.

"Oh, I promise to be very good," I told her. "Very, very good." I stroked my hand over her ass, squeezing one of the cheeks.

"Pervert," she grinned, pushing me away. "Save that for later."

We got into the car and set off for a bar where we'd arranged to meet some friends. It would be one of our typical evenings—we'd spend a couple of hours there and then go on to a club. After that, the two of us would go finally head back to my place and the real fun would really start.

"Is Marco okay," I asked, dropping the question casually into the conversation as we drove.

She looked at me strangely for a moment. "Why are you always so interested in my brother?" she asked, pulling a face.

"I just wondered," I said. "He's normally around when I pick you up, but today there was no sign of him."

She shrugged. "The little perv was up in his room. He was probably busy looking at his dirty pictures and jerking off."

I tried to ignore the sudden feeling of deep hurt which stabbed into me. *Why did I feel hurt by this?* Marco must have known I was there; he would have heard the doorbell and he must have been able to hear me and Sophia talking at the bottom of the stairs. Yet he hadn't put in even a brief appearance. This seemed to confirm my earlier suspicions: he wasn't interested in me anymore. *Oh well, if that's the way he feels, then why I should I bother?* I thought. *It's not as if he means anything to me anyway; he's been more of a nuisance than anything else. It's past time that I forget about him and get on with my life.*

Time seemed to drag in the bar. The people we were with were much more Sophia's friends than they were mine, and I felt pretty much like an outsider in most of the ongoing conversations. So many petty discussions about people I didn't know and didn't care to hear about.

I was relieved when it was time to move on to the club. We'd be with the same group of friends, of course, but at least the noise there would mean I wouldn't have to worry about having to talk to them. I could also get Sophia onto the dance floor and away from them.

It was coming up to midnight when I suggested to Sophia that we call it a night and head back to my apartment. She looked like she was about to argue, but then changed her mind and agreed. Once we were alone in the car I decided to mention something that I'd been thinking about for most of the evening.

"I want you to move in with me," I said.

There was open surprise on Sophia's face. Then she laughed. "You're kidding? You mean you want me to move into your apartment?"

"Yeah. What's so funny about that?' I shook my head. "You keep telling me that you love me, and I definitely love you. Let's do it."

She stopped laughing, and now a look of uncertainty crossed her face. "I don't know," she said.

"You are serious about us aren't you? You keep telling me you are."

"Of course I'm serious. It just, well, moving in together is such a big step."

"It is when you refuse to even spend the night with me," I said, allowing some of my annoyance to show through.

She was silent a moment, as if thinking my request over, and then she nodded. "Alright," she said. "I'll move in with you. But not until after my eighteenth birthday."

"Why should that make a difference?"

She leaned against my arm and reached up and stroked my face. "That will make it more special. It's not long; just one more week away. Surely you can wait that long."

She was right, it wasn't long to wait. Her eighteenth birthday was only eight days away. "Yeah, I can wait that long," I said, giving her an eager smile.

"Good." She set her lips into a sexy pout as she continued to stroke her fingers lightly over my lips. "And while we're on the subject of my birthday, I hope you haven't forgotten about my present."

"How could I forget?" I asked. "You remind me every single time I see you. You realise that if I spend that sort of money, we're going to have to live on bread and water for month?" I was only half-joking. Sophia had set her heart on a pair of diamond ear studs. They were expensive enough to hurt, even on my salary, and I was sure she'd picked them simply because of their price and not because she really liked them so much.

"Oh, Ed," she purred, "don't you think I'm worth it?" Her finger traced its way down the front of my shirt and past my belt, stopping at my groin. I felt her fumble for a moment with my trousers and then my zip was pulled down and she was reaching inside for my hardening cock.

"I wish you wouldn't do that while I'm driving," I sighed, trying to focus on the road. "Alright, yes you're worth it. You're worth every penny. Now stop that until we get back to my place or we're going to end up crashing into something."

She giggled, but she didn't let go of my cock, keeping her fingers wrapped tightly around the hard shaft.

It was with great relief that I finally pulled my BMW to a stop in my parking space. "Right, let's get upstairs," I told her. "I'm going to show you what happens to little girls who can't behave themselves in moving cars."

She gave my cock a final squeeze, causing me to gasp. "It's me who is going to be doing the showing," she giggled. "Tonight I'm going to wear you out."

I was late getting out of bed on Sunday morning.

Sophia had indeed tried to fulfill her threat to "wear me out", and I'd responded with a vigour and enthusiasm that had surprised even her. It was by far the hottest session we'd ever had, and any lingering doubts about my sexuality that may have been nestling in the back of my mind were now well and truly dispelled. The only fly in the ointment had been Sophia's insistence that I drive her home afterwards. I'd argued that since she would be moving in permanently in a week's time, spending the night with me would hardly hurt, but she refused to budge. One more week and I would no longer have to turn out in the middle of the night to take her home. I could hardly wait.

As I sat at the kitchen table in just my boxers, drinking my second cup of coffee, I glanced at the clock. It was almost eleven. I really ought to think about getting some clothes on and having a quick clean around before lunch. I'd decided that the cleaning could wait for a few more minutes, when I was disturbed by the door buzzer.

Wearily, I stumbled over to the door and pressed the intercom button. "Who is it?"

"It's me, Marco."

Shit! Hearing his voice instantly brought back all of those mixed emotions I thought I'd managed to lock away. I remembered that I had resolved to tell him not to come around so often, but the chances were that any such confrontation would be emotional, and I really didn't feel up to it this morning. "Marco, it's, erm, not really convenient just at the moment. I'm a bit busy."

"Edward...please open up...I need to see you." His voice was slightly distorted by the electronics of the cheap intercom unit, but even with the distortion, it was obvious that he was close to tears.

I sighed to myself. The easiest thing would be to just send him on his way, but I couldn't bring myself to do that; I couldn't make myself hurt him. *I'm just too much of a softy.* "Come on up," I said, pressing the button to release the lock on the front door.

I took the latch off my apartment door and returned to the kitchen and to my coffee mug. If I have to have an emotional confrontation, I need plenty of caffeine inside me first. I heard the door creak open. "I'm in the kitchen." I took another drink.

However, one glance at Marco standing in the kitchen doorway was enough to cause me to forget my coffee altogether. "Jesus, Marco! What the hell happened?"

He looked at me and tried to smile. One side of his mouth was dark and swollen as though he'd been punched. One eye was similarly swollen, with a large dark bruise underneath it, and there was a long graze-like scratch on his neck.

As I took a step towards the boy I saw that his eyes were filled with tears and his lips started to tremble. Automatically, I opened my arms and a moment later he was in them, his face pressed against my bare chest as he sobbed uncontrollably.

"Oh, Marco, what's happened to you?" I asked, softly. I stroked the back of his head and then moved my arms lower to give him a comforting hug. As my arms tightened, he let out a gasp of pain and I immediately let go of him. Pushing him back slightly, I lifted his shirt up.

He watched me, wordlessly, his eyes never leaving mine. A large, dark, purple bruise marred the pale skin on one side of his chest.

"Oh, Marco," I said again, "what happened to you?" Once more putting my arms around him but being careful not put any pressure on his bruised ribs. I held him until his tears stopped, by which time I was starting to feel just a bit uncomfortable. I'd given in to the impulse to comfort the boy without conscious thought, and it now felt a little strange, standing here half-naked with my arms around another guy, even if he was only seventeen. It was a relief to be able to break the contact and sit him down. I poured him a glass of orange juice and then took the seat opposite him.

"Alright, just what happened to you?" I asked, my voice soft, but at the same time insistent enough to make it clear that I wasn't going to be easily distracted.

"I don't want to talk about it," he said, looking down at his half-empty glass.

"Oh, for heaven's sake, Marco, someone has beaten the crap out of you. You can't just pretend it didn't happen. You came here looking like this! I want to know who did this to you."

"Why? You want to go beat them up?" He looked at me sadly.

"No, of course I don't. But you should go to the police..."

"No cops!" His sad gaze turned into a hard glare.

"Okay, no cops. But I still want to know what happened."

He shook his head. "I told you, I don't want to talk about it."

"You don't want to talk about it, yet you came here to see me." I was at a loss. *What am I supposed to do now?* "Let me get some clothes on, and I'll take you home," I told him getting up from the table.

"No!" He jumped up and then gave a gasp of pain, his bruised ribs protesting against the sudden movement.

I stopped, and putting my hand out to him, I gently pressed him back down into his seat and stood looking at him. "Look, I know you don't get on well with your family, a lot of kids your age don't, but you can't hide something like this from your mother; she has to know."

"She already knows," he said, quietly, not looking at me.

"She does?" Now I was feeling a little silly. I'd been all ready to leap into action and try and sort things out for him and it now appeared that everything had already been taken care of. "When did this happen?" I asked.

"Yesterday."

"Yesterday? But if..." My words trailed off, but I completed the sentence in my head. If it happened yesterday, then Sophia must have known about her brother's condition when I'd asked her if Marco was okay. *Why didn't she tell me? Did she really care so little about him that she thought something like this not worth mentioning?* "I'm surprised your mother didn't insist on calling the police in," I said.

"I've told you before, she doesn't care about me."

"Don't be silly. Of course she cares."

He glared at me again. "You don't know anything."

I ignored this. "I'd still like to know who did this to you," I said. Then I remembered what Sophia had told me, the first time I'd mentioned Marco's bruises to her. "Marco, you didn't get these from trying to pick up guys, did you?"

The boy's eyes flashed with a sudden fire. "What do you mean, pick up guys?" he asked. There was a warning tone in his voice, but I plunged ahead anyway.

"You know what I mean. Picking up guys for sex and stuff."

He got to his feet again, but slowly this time. He was shaking with suppressed anger. "Is that what you think I do?"

"I don't know," I said trying to conciliatory. "I just thought it might be something like that because you hear about those sorts of things all the time; gays getting beaten up, and Sophia said..."

"Sophia said? You listened to that lying cow?" He was backing towards the door and there were fresh tears on his face. "You think just because I'm gay I'm going to try to go with just anyone? You really think I'm like that?"

"Marco..." I reached out for him, but he pushed me away.

"I thought you were my friend! I thought you were different to all the others."

"Marco, I am your friend."

"Yeah, sure. Some friend you are if you think I would do something like that." He was past the kitchen door now. "I should have known better than to trust you. You're no different from any of the others." He turned to leave.

This looked to be turning out pretty badly. I grabbed for his arm and catching him by the wrist I pulled him towards me. He tried to fight me off but I hauled him close and put my arms around him, holding him.

"Get off me. Leave me alone."

"Marco, stop it! Stop it now!" I raised my voice to a shout.

He froze, looking up at me with wide eyes. "I didn't do anything like that," he said, after a long moment, his voice small. "I wouldn't. I've never even done anything with anyone."

"I know," I said, gently. "I'm sorry, I shouldn't have suggested it."

"There's no one would want to do anything with me anyway. No one cares about me." He gave a sad, forced smile and then the tears started again. Again I held him until the tears stopped, this time not feeling in the least bit uncomfortable. I realized then how unfair I had been, blaming Marco for my own problems. *Marco is gay, he can't help that.* If, for a while, I doubted my own sexuality, then that's was hardly Marco's fault, is it? Marco obviously needed a friend at the moment and it looked like I had been nominated by default. I knew I couldn't turn him away. "Marco, I'm your friend," I told him. "And I care about what happens to you. That's why I hate to see you hurt. If you don't want to tell me what happened, that's fine. But I want you to tell me that you're not in any danger and that it's not likely to happen again."

Marco looked at me a moment in silence and then he shook his head. "It won't," he said softly.

"Okay, that's good enough for me."

Chapter Seven

Over the next few days, Marco continued to come round every day. He was always there waiting for me when I arrived home from work and, strangely, I felt myself actively looking forward to the time that we spent together. I knew he still had a bit of a crush on me, but he was always careful to try to keep this hidden, and I no longer felt threatened by my own feelings towards him. I'd placed him firmly into the "younger brother" role. Since it's okay to care about your little brother, it let me accept that it was okay for me to have a certain amount of affection for Marco.

The only real fly in the ointment was Marco's continued insistence that Sophia was no good for me. He rarely missed a chance to take a dig at her, and he was especially upset by the fact that she would be moving in this coming weekend. I'd tried to reassure him that it wouldn't make any difference to him and me and that he would still be able to keep coming round whenever he liked, but this didn't seem to convince him.

One thing that hadn't gone down well with me was a call from Sophia telling me that she wouldn't be able to see me at all this week. Not until the weekend. She said something about exams at school and that she needed to prepare for them, and I had no choice but to reluctantly accept this news. The plan now was that we'd go out as usual on Saturday. Then, on Sunday, it was her eighteenth birthday, and there was a big get together planned with all her friends to help her celebrate. I wasn't especially looking forward to the get together, but knowing that she'd agreed to move in with me on Monday would help me get through it.

The week seemed to fly by and, almost before I knew what was happening, it was Thursday. This was a day that I definitely had been looking forward too.

Marco was there waiting for me, as normal, when I arrived home, and we went up to the apartment together. I watched him drop his school bag in the kitchen, as he normally did. Then he froze as he saw what was on the kitchen table. He flashed me a sudden, surprised and delighted smile, and then turned his attention back to the card and small, wrapped parcel that sat on the table top. "What's this?" he asked.

"Well, it's your birthday in a few days, right? Since Sophia constantly reminds me that it's her birthday on Sunday, I figured out that it must be yours today. I mean, why would you want to share the spotlight with her?" I knew that I could not begin to imagine the competition which must exist between those two. "I was hoping I'd got it right, because you've never mentioned it except for that one time. Go ahead, they're for you, so get them opened."

Cautiously, as if afraid that it would bite him, Marco reached for the card. He carefully opened the envelope and pulled the card out.

I found I was holding my breath. I'd spent almost an entire lunch hour in the card shop trying to choose the right card, vacillating between whether to get a joke one or a cute one. In the end I'd acted on impulse and got one with a cuddly bear on the front and the words "To my very special friend". This now seemed a bit over soppy and I was wishing I'd gone for the joke one instead.

As Marco looked at the card, he gave a broad grin. His hands were actually shaking as he opened it. He glanced at what I'd written inside and then read it aloud. "To Marco, my number-one boy. Happy eighteenth birthday. Love from Edward." He looked up at me, his eyes filled with tears.

"Hey, it's only a silly card," I told him, feeling a little embarrassed by his emotional reaction. *I definitely should have gone with the joke card.* "Go ahead and open your present."

He carefully stood the card on the table and picked up the parcel, pulling at the wrapping paper. His eyes widened as the paper came away. "Oh, wow," he murmured. "Thanks Edward." It was an MP3 player, identical to my own.

I'd let him use mine often enough while he sat and did his schoolwork. It was a pretty good one with lots of memory and so it hadn't been cheap, but I had a friend in the business who could get them for me at cost price so it wasn't really all that bad. Besides, the look on Marco's face made it worth every penny. "I thought it would be nice if you had one of your own," I told him. "I know you don't have a computer at home, but you're here almost every day, so you can use my computer to load stuff into it."

"It's brilliant. It's the best thing ever." His arms went around me in a hug, and I hugged him back, being careful not to squeeze his ribs, which I knew were still sore.

"I'm glad you like it," I said. "We can take it through into the lounge and get some tracks loaded onto it. But first I have one more surprise for you."

"Something else?"

"Yeah."

"It's not a car is it?" he asked with a trace of his usual humour.

"No, not this year." I untangled myself from his arms and went over to the fridge.

Marco gave a delighted laugh as he watched me take out a small cake, complete with birthday candles, and a half bottle of champagne. "We've got to do things properly," I said. I put the cake onto the table and then quickly lit all the candles. "Okay, now blow them out and make a wish."

He did, his eyes shining.

All this fuss was perhaps a little bit childish, but Marco was obviously loving it, and if I were to be honest, so was I.

The cork came out of the champagne bottle with a loud pop and I poured two glasses. "Happy eighteenth birthday, Marco," I said raising one of the glasses.

"Thanks, Edward," Marco grinned, and, glass in hand, he hugged me again.

We spent the rest of the evening selecting music tracks and loading them onto Marco's new player, between times eating slices of cake and finishing off the champagne. Marco appeared happier than I had ever seen him and this in turn gave me a thrill of pleasure. At last though, it was time for him to go.

"I wish it were me moving in instead of Sophia," he said, sadly, as we made our way down to the car.

"Well, you're here so often it's almost like you live here already," I pointed out.

He went quiet for a moment, then turned his head to look at me. "If anything happens between you and Sophia, the two of us can still be friends, can't we? It will still be alright for me to keep coming round?"

I laughed. "Nothings going to happen. Besides, even if it did, why should it make any difference to me and you?"

He appeared at least partially satisfied, but he continued to look at me. "There are things about Sophia that you should know," he said.

"Marco, stop it, please. I don't want to hear it. I know you don't get on with Sophia, so let's just not talk about her, okay?"

"I wish you'd listen to me," he said, sulkily.

"Marco, that's enough."

He went quiet and his face paled. "I'm sorry," he said, his voice very soft. "I love you Edward. You're my best friend ever, and today has been my best birthday ever." There were tears on his face as he hugged me and I realized I had tears in my own eyes. "You're my only friend."

"I'm glad you enjoyed today," I told him, trying to keep my voice steady. "Come on, get in the car and I'll take you home."

Marco was uncharacteristically quiet on Friday evening. He obviously had something on his mind and I had a good idea what it was.

"You're worrying over nothing," I told the boy, as we finished our meal, during which he hadn't spoken more than a couple of words. "I've told you that Sophia moving in won't make any difference to you coming round. She can go off and do some of the things that girls do, while the two of us spend some time together." I didn't expect for one minute that the situation would lend itself to such an easy solution, and I was prepared for some protests from Sophia when I told her that her brother would be here sometimes. But she was just going to have to get used to the idea. This was going to be *our* flat after all.

Marco looked at me, his eyes cloudy. "I need to talk to you about Sophia," he said.

I sighed. "Please, Marco. I'm trying to sort things out so that everyone is happy. You're going to have to give a little. You've got to accept that Sophia and I are going to be together. I'm sure that if you both made a bit of effort, you could get along instead of constantly fighting all the time."

"Why won't you ever listen to me?" Marco demanded, shaking his head. "Sophia doesn't care about you; she never has. She's just using you.

"I've heard all of this before, Marco, and I'm sick of hearing it. Sophia is moving in with me next Monday and you can either learn to live with that or you can stay away." I was getting annoyed and my mouth was moving faster than my brain. That last bit had come out much harsher than I'd intended.

Marco looked hurt, but he remained defiant. "She's not moving in," he said.

I gave a bitter laugh. "Oh, and you're going to stop her, are you?"

"She's not moving in," Marco repeated. "She never intended to move in."

"What are you talking about?"

"She only agreed to move in with you to keep you happy, until after her birthday. As soon as you've given her those diamond things for her ears, she's going to dump you."

"What, just like that?" I gave him an incredulous look. "Yeah sure. She's going to dump me. You really need to grow up, Marco."

"Maybe not just like that," Marco admitted. "She might string it out for a few days, making excuses why she won't move in with you, but once she gets her present, you're going to get dumped."

"Oh, and I suppose she told you this."

"No. I heard her and Mum talking. They cooked it up between them. Sophia didn't even want to get back with you after that last bust-up you had, but Mum talked her into it. Mum said that since you had plenty of money, Sophia might as well stick with you until after her birthday."

"You're just talking stupid."

"Am I? Why do you think she refused to move in with you until after her birthday?"

"It was because...well, I don't know. Why should it matter?"

"You're not listening to me, Edward." Marco was getting more agitated and he was clearly upset. "She's going to hurt you. I don't want to see you hurt. I care about you even if she doesn't."

"It's not Sophia who's trying to hurt me, it's you," I replied, heatedly. Marco wasn't the only one getting upset by this unwelcome exchange. "You can't accept that it's Sophia that I'm interested in and not you. I'm straight, Marco, not gay, straight. I've tried to be nice to you and be your friend, but that's not good enough for you and you keep throwing it back in my face. Maybe," I paused for a moment, "maybe it's time you stopped coming round here."

"Okay, so you're straight," Marco said, getting to his feet, his eyes full of tears. "But that doesn't change the fact that Sophia is going to hurt you. She's already seeing someone else. That's where she was last

Friday when she said she was going out with her friends. That's why she said she couldn't see you at all this week."

"I've heard enough of this crap," I snarled, now standing up myself. "You'd better go."

"Please listen, Edward," Marco sobbed. "It's Sophia you should be mad with, not me. That's why I didn't say anything before; I knew you'd take her side. But she's going to hurt you and I don't want that to happen."

"Get out," I snapped, holding the apartment door open for him.

Marco passed me, the tears rolling down his cheeks.

The guilt I felt at seeing him like this only went to further fuel my anger.

"You don't know what Sophia and Mum are like. They're not bothered who they hurt as long as they get what they want," said Marco as he pushed the elevator button. Taking a deep breath, he walked back towards the apartment door and looked at me determinedly. "Who do you think did this?" he asked through clenched teeth, pointing to the Marcos on his face. "Who do you think did this?" He lifted his shirt and pointed to his bruised ribs.

I looked at him incredulously. "You expect me to believe that your own mother did that to you?" I gave a bitter laugh. "You really have lost it, Marco. Just go. And please, stay away from now on." I put my hand on his chest and pushed him backwards through the doorway and then closed the door in his face.

I slumped against the wall.

I was badly shaken by this unexpected confrontation. I'd known that Marco didn't like Sophia, but I'd had no idea that he would carry his vendetta against her this far. Did he really think I would be stupid enough to believe all those lies?

I walked across the living room carpet to the small wet bar poured myself a drink of something strong, trying to stop my hands from shaking. Sophia had been right about him when she'd said her brother was weird. *How did I ever come to get so involved with someone like that?*

I moved over to the sofa and sat down, tipping my head back and closing my eyes as I took deep breaths to try to calm myself as something soft and classical played on the stereo. Sophia would never do anything like Marco had described, that much I was sure of. Sure, she was no angel, and she'd done the rounds before we got together, but since then she'd been completely faithful to me. If she'd been with anyone else I would have known about it; I would have been able to tell. Besides, you can't keep anything like that a secret for long; someone would have said something to me. Yes, I was sure of it. *Someone would have told me.*

Or at least I hoped they would have told me.

I knew that Sophia flirted with a lot of guys, but that was just Sophia. There was never anything in her flirting, it was all just for fun. She'd never take it further than that.

My mind whirled on, spinning out of control, as I kept telling myself that there could not possibly be anything in Marco's wild accusations. True, they would have been quite convincing to anyone who didn't know Sophia like I did. Maybe Marco even believed them himself. Maybe he had repeated the story over and over to himself until it had become credible. Yes, I suppose it was credible. Except that Sophia would never do that to me.

But deep down in heart, I knew how wrong that was.

Sophia was indeed quite capable of doing exactly that. Slowly, feeling steadily more sick, I allowed myself to consider the possibility that some of what Marco had said may have been true. *Suppose she did have someone else?* There had been plenty of weak excuses about why she couldn't be with me. And what had been her real reason for refusing to move in with me before her birthday? "To make it more special?" *What sort of a reason was that? Could she really have someone else?* I had to know. I had to find out for sure one way or the other. But how was I to find out? I could hardly ask Sophia. I mulled over the problem for a while, sipping on the neat whisky in my glass, letting the heat from the alcohol calm my nerves. And then the answer hit me.

Angelo.

No one collected gossip like Angelo. He always knew every sordid detail about who was cheating on who. If anyone knew about Sophia playing away, it would be Angelo.

With trembling hands, I flipped through my cellphone's address book and found Angelo's mobile number. I dialed.

"You have reached the ever-amazing Angelo Kristophos." Angelo's familiar effeminate tones came through the receiver as clearly as if he was standing next to me.

"Angelo, it's Edward."

"Oh, hello there handsome." He sounded even more effeminate now. "Surely you're not ready yet for me to work my magic on your beautiful locks. Or maybe that cute little boyfriend of yours wants to see me again?"

"Angelo, I need a favour."

"Ooh, how could I possibly refuse? Ask away."

"I want to know if Sophia has been seeing anyone behind my back."

The sudden silence coming through the phone told me all I needed to know. I felt molten lead settle in my stomach.

When Angelo spoke, he sounded strangely masculine; all the effeminate inflections were gone from his voice. "I'm sorry, Edward. I always told you she was no good."

"How long has it been going on?" I asked.

There was a sigh from the speaker. "As far as I know, she's never stopped seeing other guys."

"Who? Give me names."

"You sure you really want to know?"

"Yeah."

"Recently there has been Dave Morris and Dan Greenwall. I think it's Dan she's seeing at the moment."

I ground my teeth in helpless fury and frustration. I didn't know anyone called Dave Morris, but Dan was in our immediate circle of friends; he'd been one of the friends we'd met at the bar the previous Saturday. I felt like a complete fool. "Thanks, Angelo," I managed to get out.

"I'm really sorry, Edward. You're well rid of her. You going to be okay?"

"Yeah, I'll be fine. Thanks again, Angelo."

"No problem, Edward. You take care. Call me anytime you need a shoulder to cry on...or any other body part you wish to borrow."

"Yeah, thanks." Numbly, I turned off the phone and felt it slip through my fingers onto the floor. I had been so stupid. *Why had she done this to me? I'd always been there for her. I'd given her everything she'd asked for. Why?* I felt a burning rage building in my stomach, ready to explode but with nowhere to go. "Why?" I screamed out, to the empty room. An overwhelming wave of self-pity washed over me. I sank down to my knees. My back against the wall, I put my face in my hands and I began to cry.

I don't recall very much of what happened after that, except that I hit the bottle pretty hard. I do remember ringing Sophia at some point and telling her in no uncertain terms what I thought about her. The conversation quickly turned into a screaming match over the telephone and I called her a "stupid bitch" and turned off the phone and flung it across the room. I then drank some more and somehow made it to my bed, where I passed out.

Chapter Eight

I awoke on Saturday morning, sprawled across my bed, still fully dressed, and feeling like death warmed over. Just raising my head was enough to cause nausea to wash over me in waves and I had to literally crawl down the hallway to the bathroom. I used the sink to slowly pull myself to my feet and I blearily looked at myself in the bathroom mirror. Damn. I even looked like death. This study of my appearance was interrupted by an extra powerful attack of nausea and I dropped to my knees, my head over the toilet bowl. It was several minutes before I felt able to let go of the toilet bowl and once more pull myself up to the sink to splash cold water over my face.

God, I felt rough.

With an effort, I pulled off my rumpled clothes and turned on the shower, making the water as hot as I thought I would be able to stand it, and then I climbed into the bath, where I lay letting the scalding water splash down over my body.

Eventually I plucked up the courage to pull myself out of the bath and, wrapping a towel around my waist, I managed to stagger into the kitchen. I poured myself a glass of juice, restricting myself to small sips. I knew it would be a while yet before I was ready to face life.

Work was definitely out of the question. I normally work for a few hours on Saturday afternoons, but today I had no choice but to call in sick. Hell, I was sick, quite literally.

As the hours passed, I started to feel a little bit more human.

Unfortunately, as the physical discomfort eased, the emotional pain of the previous day was quick to take its place. I was angry. More angry than I had ever been before. I realized now that I didn't love Sophia; I never had. But she'd made a fool of me, and that hurt. I'd clearly meant nothing at all to her. I'd just been someone for her to use and throw away. How could anyone possibly be that callous? Marco had tried to warn me. He'd told me time and again what she was like, but I'd refused to listen to him. But if he knew what was going on, he should have told me; he should have made me listen.

Part of this was his fault. I was well rid of the two of them.

By mid afternoon, I was starting to feel a little bit better and I gave myself a shave and a proper tidy up and pulled on some old and comfortably worn-in jeans and tee-shirt. I was starting to feel almost human. I didn't feel ready to face the world yet, but at least I was making progress.

I realized I hadn't eaten anything since the previous evening and decided that getting some food inside me might make me feel better.

Looking in the fridge, I came across the plate containing a small piece of Marco's birthday cake. An image flashed into my mind of Marco, laughing happily as he'd blown out the candles on his cake and then closing his eyes to make a wish. I felt a sudden painful pang of regret that this business with Sophia had caused me to lose Marco as well. Ignoring the lump in my throat, I forced myself to cross the kitchen and tip the remaining cake into the bin. I discovered that I'd lost whatever appetite I'd had. I wasn't hungry after all.

Listlessly, I wandered around the apartment.

To pass the time, I tried listening to music and watching TV, but I really wasn't in the mood for anything, and for some reason, everything I did reminded me of Marco. Even when I tried to lose myself in something mundane, like cleaning, I recalled the time just a few weeks previously, when Marco had insisted on helping me with the job. It was hard to believe that it was not even a month since I'd found him lying semi-conscious in the park, stinking of his own piss and vomit. I'd brought him back and cleaned him up and bedded him down for the night in my own bedroom, never realizing that over the next weeks he would become such an integral part of almost every aspect of my life.

I knew now that in those weeks, Marco had come to mean much more to me than Sophia ever had. Sophia had been great in bed, but beyond that, she had been nothing special. Marco had been so much more. I felt my stomach tighten as I remembered some of the things I'd said to the boy as I'd pushed him out of my apartment the previous evening. I'd told him to keep away. I'd laughed at him. Yet everything he'd said had turned out to be true. I played through what I could recall of that conversation. It hurt, but I felt the need to punish myself both for my own stupidity and for the way I'd treated the boy. He'd said that he loved me, and somehow I knew that he'd meant it. But how did I feel about him? I really didn't know. I did know that picturing him in my mind caused my stomach to knot up, and the thought of not seeing him again made me feel sick.

Almost before I realized what I was doing, I hunted down the phone from where I'd thrown it the previous evening. Luckily it didn't appear damaged. If I could just talk to Marco and tell him that I was sorry...

I hit the speed dial button.

"Hello?" It was Helena, of course.

"Helena, it's Edward."

"Oh. What do you want?" There was ice in her words and I couldn't help but picture the sneer on her face.

"I want to speak to Marco."

She gave a cold laugh. "Why doesn't that surprise me? He can't come to the phone right now. So go to hell!" She slammed down the phone.

I turned off my own phone, feeling my hands shake. I suppose it was the response I should have expected. Helena would refuse to let me speak to Marco just to spite me. I decided that maybe I would try again later and hope that Marco himself would answer. Though thinking back, in all of the times I'd called the house, I couldn't recall a single occasion where Marco had ever answered the phone. Helena had said "Why doesn't that surprise me?" almost as if she'd expected me to ask for Marco. But as far as Sophia and her mother knew, I'd never had anything to do with Marco. Even when I'd taken him home I'd dropped him at the end of Grove street. Why would Helena be expecting me to ask to speak to Marco? Unless they had somehow found out that it was Marco who told me about Sophia. I sure wouldn't like to be in his shoes if that were the case.

It hit me.

"Oh, shit!"

Then I slumped back onto the couch as it really hit me.

All those bruises. Marco had said he got them from his mother. I'd laughed at him, not believing it. But what if he'd been telling the truth? I knew Helena could be a vicious cow; I'd seen it myself. And I knew what a temper Sophia had, and that she'd resort to violence if she really lost it, since I'd been on the receiving end. *What if they had hurt Marco?*

I'd picked up my leather jacket and was halfway to the door before I managed to catch myself. *What the hell was I doing? I could hardly go barging in there and start throwing accusations of abuse like that.*

I threw my jacket aside and forced myself to calm down and try to think things through. I was probably letting my imagination run away with itself. And besides, after the way I'd treated Marco, he probably wouldn't want to see me anyway. Maybe I'd misunderstood what Helena had said. If I were to go round there and insist on speaking to Marco, they were bound to realize there was some connection between us and that would probably make things worse for him.

No, it was better to wait and see what happened. I'd give things a chance to calm down, and tomorrow I'd try to find a way of contacting Marco. I could watch for him on the way home from school.

However, as the evening wore on, I found myself unable to think of anything else. Those bruises that Marco had had on his face, arms and chest had been pretty bad. Suppose he had been telling the truth and they really had been caused by his mother? He'd been telling the truth about everything else. And he'd been beaten on at least two occasions that I knew of. If she'd done it twice, she could do it again.

I glanced at the clock. It was coming up on eleven. It was getting late and I should drag myself off to bed.

It was no good though—I had to know that Marco was okay.

I grabbed my leather jacket and headed for the car.

By the time I reached Marco's house, I'd wound myself up into a real state. I marched up to the door and rang the bell, then, for good measure, I pounded on the door with my fist.

The door was opened a moment later by Sophia. "Ed?" She seemed surprised to see me. She was wearing a low-cut top and a tight skirt.

I pushed her aside and stepped into the hallway.

Dan Greenwall was there. It looked like the two of them had been just about to go out. Given the way they were dressed, they were probably on their way to a club. *It's nice to know Sophia isn't taking our break-up too hard.* At least Dan had the good graces to look uncomfortable by my arrival.

"Don't worry," I told Dan. "You're welcome to her. I hope you've got deep pockets though, because she'll only stay with you until she gets a better offer, and then she'll be moving on to the next poor bastard. Though in terms of dollars per fuck, she probably works out cheaper than picking up a girl off the street," I added, giving Sophia a cold look.

She glared back at me. "What the fuck do you want, Edward?" she asked.

"I want to see Marco."

"What's the matter, can't keep up with the girls so you've decided to try your luck with little boys?"

"If all the girls were like you, I'd be better off gay," I snapped back at her.

"What's going on?" Helena had appeared at the far end of the hallway. She looked at me and her mouth tightened.

"I've come to see Marco," I told her.

"Well you can't, so get out."

I ignored her and stepped towards the stairs, but she moved to intercept me.

"Marco!" I called up the stairs.

Helena got in front of me and tried to push me back.

"Marco!"

"Get out!" Helena was shouting, into my face. "Get out of my house!"

Sophia was shouting something from behind me and I felt someone grab my arm. I shook the hand off.

"Get out, or I'm calling the police," Helena screeched.

It had turned into quite a tussle. I was fighting to get to the stairs, and Helena was trying to push me back towards the door. Sophia had grabbed me again and was yanking at my arm. Poor Dan just stood and looked on, probably wondering what he had madness gotten himself into.

"Marco," I shouted again.

"Edward?" Marco appeared at the top of the stairs.

"Oh my God" i swore.

He was wearing just a pair of tatty-looking cotton shorts that were ripped all the way up one side and appeared to be held together by little more than a few threads. There were obvious fresh bruises on his arms and chest, and what looked like dried blood on one of his shoulders. There was also a cut on his face above one of his eyes and bruises on his shins as if he'd been kicked. He leaned on the stair rail for support.

"Get back in your room," Helena ordered him.

"Get out of my way," I snarled at her, grabbing her arm and flinging her aside. Seeing the state that Marco was in had confirmed my worst suspicions and no one was going to stand in my way now. I charged up the stairs.

"Sophia, call the police," I heard Helena call out.

"Yes, Sophia, call the cops," I shouted back down the stairs. "I think they should see this. In fact, I might call them myself so we can have a proper chat with you about your son."

At least Helena twitched at that threat.

Dan said nothing.

Then I turned my attention back to Marco. The boy was trembling and there were tears on his face. As soon as I reached the top of the stairs he fell into my arms. "Oh God, Marco, why did you let them do this to you? Why didn't you tell me what was happening?" I knew that he had told me, in the end, and that I'd laughed at him.

He didn't reply, he just pressed his face against my shoulder, crying.

I took a couple of deep breaths and tried to think. I'd had no plan beyond ensuring that Marco was okay, and so I had no idea where to go from here. "Marco, you can't stay here," I told him, making a snap decision. "You can't let them keep doing this to you."

Marco lifted his head and looked up at me with blank eyes.

"I'm taking you home with me," I told him. "You can stay with me until you decide what you want to do. Let's get your things." I glanced down the stairs. Helena and Sophia were standing at the bottom, both of them looked furious, but both just stood there and watched in silence.

Dan had taken a step towards the still-open door.

Silently, Marco led the way into his bedroom though he stopped just inside the doorway.

I stepped up behind him. "Holy shit!" It looked like a tornado had swept through the room.

Anything that could be broken or smashed, had been. A wardrobe standing against the far wall, stood open with its door hanging off, drawers had been ripped out and slung around, and even the curtains had been ripped away from the window. But that wasn't the half of it. The floor was littered with torn and shredded clothing, much of it ripped into several pieces. There was nothing in any better condition than the shorts that Marco was wearing.

I let out a slow breath. "Who ever did this sure did a thorough job," I murmured.

"Most of it was Sophia," said Marco, his voice trembling. "After I told her it was me who told you about what she planned to do."

"What did you go and do that for?" I asked him.

"I wanted to get back at her because of everything she's done to me. And because of what she was doing to you."

"Oh, Marco," I said, shaking my head. I hastily took off my leather jacket and put it around his shoulders and then I put my arm around him. "Come on, there's nothing here worth saving. I'll lend you something to wear until we can get you some things of your own." I started to lead him out of the door, but he pulled away from me.

"Wait." He stepped over to the mattress that lay on the floor—no bed frame, just a mattress on the floor—and lifted a corner and pulled out what looked to be pieces of torn card. He held these tightly against his chest as he came back to me. "Right," he said taking a deep breath, "I'm ready to go."

Helena stood at the bottom of the stairs, blocking our way, a determined look on her face.

I was equally determined as I slowly walked down towards her. "Marco is coming with me. You can either get out of my way, or I'll knock you flat." She looked at me uncertainly for a moment as if trying to gauge whether my threat was serious and then she gave way. It was a wise move on her part, because the mood I was in, I probably would have happily punched her. I glared at her as I walked past, keeping Marco pulled close to me.

The boy was trembling again.

When we reached the front door, I looked back at Helena and Sophia. I dearly wanted to say something to them, but couldn't think of anything that would show the utter contempt I felt for them. Instead, I spoke to Dan, who was standing well back from the scene, his face pale. "I wish you luck," I told him. "You're going to need it. You're going to need all the luck in the world."

With that, we left the house.

Marco didn't speak during the short drive back to my apartment. He was so quiet that I wondered if he had fallen asleep. However he was awake enough when we arrived to be able to give me a smile; it was a bit forced, but at least it was an improvement on earlier. I put my arm around his shoulders again and we went up to my apartment. Luckily we didn't meet anyone else in the building. It would certainly have caused some raised eyebrows if anyone had seen me sneaking in with a beaten, near-naked teenager in my arms. Inside, I led Marco directly to the guest room. It wasn't very big, but it was comfortable enough. "You can sleep in here," I told him.

Marco, nodded. "Thanks, Edward," he said. "You get into bed and I'll find you some clothes for the morning."

"Okay. Do you have any Scotch tape?"

"Yeah, I expect so. I'll dig you some out tomorrow."

"No. I need it tonight." There was something in his eyes that told me that for some reason, this was important to him.

"Okay, I'll get it for you."

When I returned to the bedroom with the requested Scotch tape and some clothes that I thought wouldn't look too bad on him, Marco was already in bed. The tattered shorts that he had worn lay on the floor. He'd turned off the main light and the room was lit only by the dim glow of the bedside lamp.

"Here you go," I said, as I handed him the tape and put the clothes onto a chair so that they would be ready for him in the morning. "Is there anything else you need?"

"No." He shook his head, sleepily.

"Alright. Get some sleep and we'll talk about all of this in the morning. Everything will seem a bit clearer then. Don't worry about anything at all, because you're going to be safe now."

Marco gave me a trembling smile and nodded. "Thanks Edward," he said.

I gently patted his shoulder. "Goodnight Marco."

"Goodnight."

I couldn't sleep. I was too wound up and angry. I'd tried forcing myself to relax, but it was no good. So many different things kept going through my head: my relationship with Sophia, how I felt about Marco, what Sophia and Helena had done to Marco, what Marco was going to do now; everything was a mixed up blur. I realized that by bringing Marco back here, I'd taken on some sort of responsibility for taking care of him, at least in the short term. *But what was going to happen after that?* Was he going to stay with me on a longer term basis? *Did he want to?* I recalled Marco saying recently that he wished he could move in with me, but how serious had he really been? Did I want him here all the time?

So many questions and no answers.

Marco was practically eighteen now, so as long as his mother didn't cause problems, there was nothing to stop him staying with me, and if Helena decided to be difficult about it she would be stirring up a huge amount of trouble for herself.

The more I thought about the idea of Marco moving in with me permanently, the more I liked the idea. There would be some problems, of course, but nothing that we couldn't sort out. He would be completely financially dependent on me, but even living here full time he'd probably cost me less than Sophia had done in the time I'd been seeing her. I soon managed to convince myself that Marco staying here would be the ideal solution.

It was definitely what I wanted.

But what if Marco had other ideas? I felt a sudden twist of fear at the idea that Marco might decide that he didn't want to stay with me. Though what scared me even more, was my reaction to that thought. Why did the thought of losing Marco bother me so much? My heart started to beat faster as I vividly recalled the time that the two of us had almost kissed, and in my mind the scene continued to its natural conclusion; this time I didn't pull back, and Marco's lips on mine were soft and sweet.

Damn! I shook my head to remove the picture and forced myself to think of so*mething else. Surely this couldn't be healthy; I was becoming infatuated with a seventeen-year-old boy. Was this some sort of reaction to my splitting up with Sophia?* I knew it wasn't. I'd felt this way about Marco while Sophia was still on the scene, even though I'd refused to let myself think about it at the time. Maybe, just maybe, considering my confused feelings towards Marco, the best thing for both of us would be for him not to stay with me after all.

I ground my teeth in helpless frustration. I was going around in circles. *Let him stay, or not let him stay?* I didn't know what the hell to do.

On impulse, I decided to check that the boy was okay. I climbed out of bed, straightening my silk boxers, which had become twisted as a result of all the restless tossing and turning, and made my way silently down the short hallway to Marco's room. The door was slightly ajar, and I could see that the bedside lamp was still on. Pushing the door open, I stepped inside.

Marco lay half on his side, apparently asleep. The bedclothes were pulled up around his chest, and both arms lay bare, on top of the sheets. Quietly, I moved closer until I was standing over him. I could tell now that he was indeed asleep; his was face relaxed and peaceful. As I stood watching him, I felt a strange tightness in my chest. He was so beautiful; even the bruises on his face and upper arms did nothing to detract from that. He looked so peaceful and innocent, that I couldn't imagine how anyone could possibly bring themselves to hurt him. Then I noticed what he held in his hand and my breath caught in my throat. It was the birthday card I'd given him. This was what he had wanted the tape for. The card had been torn into pieces, but Marco had carefully reassembled them and taped them back together. He'd fallen asleep with the repaired card gripped in his hand, and it lay open with the words I'd written inside clearly on display. "To Marco, my number one boy. Happy ninteenth birthday. Love from Edward."

I turned away, my eyes brimming with tears. "Oh, Marco," I murmured. "What am I going to do?" I sighed deeply. I had to get a grip. I needed to get some sleep and maybe things would be clearer in the morning. Wiping the tears from my face, I moved silently back to my own room and climbed back into bed. Eventually I fell into a restless sleep.

Chapter Nine

"Edward? You awake?"

Marco's voice brought me out of my light doze. I'd been awake for a while, but had been putting off getting up. "Erm, yeah. I guess so," I replied, giving a yawn. I lifted myself up onto one elbow and sleepily scratched at my head.

Marco peered at me from around my bedroom door, just his head and one bare shoulder visible.

"You want me?" I asked.

"I was just wondering if it was okay for me to get a shower."

"Of course it is. You don't need to ask; just go ahead."

"I would have," he said, "only there's no towel."

"Ah, yeah, sorry." I now remembered putting the dirty towels into the washing machine the previous evening. I'd meant to replace them with clean ones but it must have slipped my mind. *No surprise given my mental state this weekend.* "I'll get you one. Go get your shower and I'll bring you one in."

Marco disappeared and I forced myself to get out of bed, stretching my muscles. Then, barefooted and wearing just my boxers, I padded through to the kitchen to get some clean towels from where they were stored in the cupboard above the hot water tank.

As I entered the bathroom, I could hear the sound of the running shower. "I got your towel, Marco," I called, feeling a strange momentary pang of disappointment that he had pulled the shower curtain across and was hidden behind it.

"Okay, thanks Edward. I won't be long."

"No rush. It's here when you want it." I contemplated waiting here until Marco pulled back the curtain, but quickly got control of myself. *What am I doing?* I put the towel on the rail and went back to the kitchen, where I tried once more to make sense of what I was feeling. I'd actually gone into that bathroom hoping to catch a glimpse of Marco naked. *What the hell is the matter with me?* My hand trembled as I poured myself a glass of water.

Marco followed me into the kitchen a couple of minutes later. He had an orange towel wrapped around his waist and he held it in place by gripping the corners at his side. His hair was wet and their were droplets of water on his shoulders and chest.

I gave him a smile, which he returned. For some reason, his smile made my heart beat faster. "How do you feeling this morning?" I asked him.

"Okay, I guess. A bit sore." Marco touched lightly at the scabbed-over cut above his eye.

"Here, let me look at that." I stepped up to him and put my hands one to each side of his face as I peered closely at the swollen area on the side of his forehead. The skin of his face felt so soft to my touch. "It doesn't look too bad," I said after examining it. "Which one of them gave you that?" I immediately felt him tense up at the question. This was obviously something he didn't want to talk about, but at the same time it was something we couldn't ignore.

"Mum did it," he said, a tremor in his voice. "I was on the floor and she kicked me."

"She kicked you in the face?" I looked at him completely dumbfounded, my mind refusing to accept that any mother could do that to one of her children.

"At least she missed my mouth this time," said Marco, with an extremely forced smile.

"Oh, Marco. Why didn't you tell someone what was happening? Why did you stay there and let her keep doing it?"

He gave an unhappy shrug. "What would they have done if I'd told someone? Either they would have given her a warning, which would have made her hate me even more, or I would have been taken into care."

"Surely even that would have been better than having her treat you like that."

"You think so? You ever been in care? I spent three months in a children's home when I was twelve; it was awful."

"You could have run away."

"I did...how do you think I ended up in care?"

"Oh. I spoke without thinking."

Marco sighed. "I did runaway again when I was fifteen...got brought home by the cops. They saw the bruises...mum said they were from the lowlifes I was hanging out with on the streets."

"I'm sorry."

"Better to just lay low at home. I had school to get me out of the house part of the day. More food than living on the street. Besides, she didn't hit me all the time. It was only sometimes. I tried to keep out of her way most of the time, and I kept telling myself that maybe it wouldn't happen again." He went quiet, then lifted his eyes to look up into mine. "What's going to happen to me now?" he asked, clearly on the verge of tears.

"Nothing," I told him firmly. "You're staying here with me; as long as you want to, anyway. You're eighteen now. Adult. So as long as you're safe, I don't think anyone would be interested unless your mother decides to make a fuss. If she causes any trouble then we can go to the police and tell them what's been happening to you."

"I don't want the cops involved," Marco said quickly. "I don't want everybody knowing about it."

"Don't worry. We won't go to them unless we have to. I can't see Helena wanting to cause a scene either."

"You really mean it, I can stay here?" Marco looked at me hopefully.

"Yeah, I mean it. You're my number-one boy right?" That last part came out without thinking, intended to cheer Marco up. It certainly did the job.

"Oh, Edward, thank you." Marco gave me a one-armed hug, his other hand still engaged in stopping his orange towel from falling to the floor.

I hugged him in return, and we stood for several long seconds with our bare chests pressed together, my hands running lightly over the smooth, soft skin of his back. It felt incredible.

"I think you ought to go get dressed, Marco," I said, eventually. "We've got a busy day ahead. We need to go out and get you some clothes."

He looked at me worriedly. "I haven't got any money. I wasn't allowed to have a job. I haven't got anything at all."

"It's not a problem," I smiled. "I'll get you everything you need."

"You can't keep spending money on me."

"Oh yes I can. Sophia never worried about spending my money."

"I'm not Sophia!"

"I know you're not," I said, gently stroking his cheek. "Go and get your clothes on."

As Marco went back to the guest room to get dressed, I went into the bathroom to take my own shower.

My mind was still in turmoil and I was more confused than I'd ever been before. I was feeling things for Marco that I had never felt for Sophia; things that I had never felt for anyone else at all. It wasn't so much physical things, it was much more emotional. I wanted to take care of Marco, to comfort him when he was upset, to be with him all the time. But it went beyond that. There seemed to be an almost constant desire for physical contact, like the way I had just stroked his cheek; it had been an impulse gesture, but that sort of contact went way beyond simple friendship. It wasn't just the fact that Marco was a guy, though that was disturbing enough. There was also the small matter of me being an adult and Marco still being a teen; feelings of this sort weren't natural. I gave a wry smile as it occurred to me that Marco was eighteen now. Sophia had only been seventeen and I'd thought nothing of fucking her brains out for half the night. It was a matter of perception: Sophia had always been experienced well beyond her years, and Marco had none of that experience and seemed surrounded by an aura of innocence and vulnerability.

My breath caught as I realized the direction my thoughts had taken. I had actually been happily contemplating some sort of sexual experience with Marco.

A wave of guilt washed over me. *This wasn't right.* I immediately banished all improper thoughts from my head and tried to concentrate on more practical matters. I began making a mental list of what we would need to buy today.

I had always enjoyed shopping. There is something therapeutic about wandering around the stores buying nice clothes. However, I'd never enjoyed it so much as I had today. Shopping with Marco took things to a whole new level. The teen had at first been reluctant to spend money, apparently satisfied with the cheapest items he could find, but I was having none of that.

In spite of being a bit on the thin side, Marco was a great-looking kid; even more so now that Angelo had sorted his hair out. I knew that with the right clothes, he wouldn't just look great—he would look incredible and, for some reason, this was really important to me.

Maybe I am shallow?

Marco had eventually given in, not that he'd had any choice in the matter, and he'd even started to enjoy the experience. He clung to his usual fashions—some new jeans, hoodies—but I got him a few polo shirts and some slacks. One of our first stops had been to get him some new sneakers—we'd gone out with him wearing one of my old pairs and they were too large for him. We had already been back to the car with one load of bags and we were still going strong.

Our next port of call was the jewellers. This was something I hadn't been looking forward to, but it had to be done. And the sooner the better. I had previously paid a deposit on the diamond ear studs that were to have been Sophia's eighteenth birthday present, and I had been supposed to call into the shop yesterday to pay the balance and collect the studs. That was before things had taken an unexpected turn. I gave the store assistant a short explanation of the situation and she was about to refund my deposit when, out of the corner of my eye, I noticed Marco looking at a display case containing watches. I gave the assistant a signal to hold off for a moment and went over to the boy.

"See anything you like?" I asked, casually.

"Yeah, loads," he grinned. He looked around. "You finished."

"Almost," I told him. "Which one do you like the best?"

"That one," he laughed, pointing to a nice looking watch. It had a segmented stainless steel strap with gold coloured highlights, and a round face, again highlighted with a gold colour. It was priced at a hundred and twenty, one of the more expensive ones in that particular display case.

I waved to the assistant to come over. "Can we have a look at this one?" I asked her.

"What are you doing?" Marco asked me, a look of worried disbelief on his face.

I ignored him and accepted the watch from the assistant. Taking hold of Marco's hand, I slipped the watch over it and closed it around his wrist. It looked good against his olive skin. "You like it?" I asked the boy.

"Yeah, of course I like it. But..."

"It's a bit loose," I told the assistant. "Can you adjust it?"

"No problem," the assistant smiled. "We can take a couple of links out of the strap. It'll just take a minute."

"Great. We'll take it. Use the deposit from the studs and I'll pay the balance."

"OK, I'll just need to take it through to the back for a minute so that we can take these links out for you." The assistant disappeared through a doorway.

"What are you doing?" Marco hissed at me, his eyes flicking towards the door of the store as though we were doing something wrong and he was checking his escape route.

"I'm buying you a watch," I told him, with a grin.

"But you can't," he insisted. "It's too much money."

I gave a shrug. "You like it, so it doesn't matter how much it costs. Look, if it makes you feel any better, think of it as a reward for all the money you saved me by telling me about Sophia."

"I don't want a reward. Not for that."

"Well think of it as a gift then."

"But..."

"Marco, I'm buying you the watch and that's the end of the matter."

Marco gave me a stubborn glare and he looked so sweet that I had to struggle to stop myself from hugging him.

The assistant returned with the adjusted watch and I once more put it on Marco's wrist to try it for size. It fit perfectly.

"He'll keep it on. Put the box in a bag for me," I told the girl, handing her the balance of the money.

Marco continued to glare as we left the shop. However, as we walked along, I noticed him admiring the watch on his wrist, a look of delight on his face. He glanced up at me, catching me grinning at him.

"What's so funny?" he demanded.

"You are," I laughed. I briefly put my arm around his shoulders, giving him a squeeze.

It was already well passed lunch time and we hadn't eaten since breakfast, so I suggested we get something to eat, and Marco readily agreed. We found a small cafe and bought some sandwiches and some drinks.

As we ate, I noticed that Marco had gone very quiet.

"You okay?" I asked him.

He looked at me. "Were you really serious when you said I could stay with you?"

"I told you I was. Marco, you've got nothing to worry about on that score. You can stay with me for as long as you want; I like having you around."

"But what happens when you get yourself another girlfriend? Suppose you want her to move in? You won't want me there then; I'll be in the way."

I didn't know what to say. This was something I hadn't even considered. Sophia was hardly out of the door, and I was still smarting, so I had given no thought at all to future relationships. Besides that, I was having serious problems trying to sort out my feelings towards Marco. "Maybe I won't get another girlfriend," I said, rather lamely.

"Yeah, right."

"Whatever happens, I'm not going to kick you out. I've got two bedrooms, and if I do have a girl move in with me, she'll be sleeping with me, so that will still leave one for you."

"I'll be in the way though."

"You won't. Marco, stop it." I was starting to get annoyed, though the annoyance was more with myself than with Marco. He was right, I really hadn't thought any of this through. I had been avoiding thinking about the longer term, and I still didn't want to think about it. Everything seemed far too mixed up and confused for me to look at anything beyond the immediate future.

My tone had been harsher than I'd intended and Marco lapsed back into silence. He sat staring at his plate, playing with his food. I wanted to say sorry, but that seemed pretty pointless unless I could add some sort of explanation, and at the moment I couldn't do that. "Come on,"

I said getting to my feet. "I don't think either of us are that hungry, and there are still some things that we need to get."

I waited for Marco to get up and then followed him out of the cafe.

As we stepped out into the street, Marco suddenly stopped dead, frozen in his tracks, and I stumbled into him. As I stepped round him, I shot a puzzled glance at his face and saw that it had completely drained of colour and that he was staring across the street. I followed his gaze.

Helena and Sophia were walking towards us. Helena had a bitter smile on her face.

I glanced back at Marco. His eyes were still fixed on his mother and sister and he had started to tremble. He was terrified. I deliberately stepped in front of him, blocking his view and, putting my hands to each side of his head, I forced him to look directly into my eyes. "Marco, listen to me. They can't hurt you. I won't let them hurt you. You're safe. You don't have to speak to them. You don't even have to look at them. Just ignore them. I'll take care of it."

Marco gave a small nod and swallowed nervously.

I gave him a smile that I didn't feel and tenderly stroked his cheek, noting absently that this was the second time today that I had made that intimate gesture. Then, taking a quick breath to steel myself, I turned around to face Helena and Sophia.

"Well, look who it is," Helena sneered.

"You want something, Helena?"

"Not from you," the woman replied. "Though I can't help wondering why you're taking such an interest in a young boy; I'm sure a lot of people would wonder the same thing."

"Let them wonder," I replied. "If they ask, I'll tell them. And I'll also tell them that his mother is an evil bitch who used him as a punching bag. Maybe the police would be interested in seeing the bruises he's got all over him. You make any trouble, Helena, and I swear you'll come off much worse than I will."

"Don't threaten me," she said. "It would be his word against mine."

"You want to try it and see who they would believe? I think the bruises speak for themselves."

She started to look uncertain. "He didn't get anything he didn't deserve."

"One of these days, hopefully you'll get what you deserve," I said, trying to keep a grip on my building anger. "If you do anything else at all to try to hurt Marco, I'll make you very sorry."

Helena must have picked up the sincerity in my voice, because she stepped back a pace. "You're welcome to him," she muttered. "He'd better keep away from my house; I don't want to see him there again. I don't want anything else to do with him." Her voice was like ice.

Marco was behind me, so I couldn't see his reaction to this, but I could imagine how he must feel. Hearing these words from his own mother must have been every bit as painful as a kick in the ribs.

I felt my anger redouble and I clenched my fists at my sides. "You really are evil. I don't know how you can live with yourself," I snarled. I looked from Helena to Sophia. "Like mother, like daughter; you two really do deserve each other. Where's Dan, Sophia? Has he seen through you already?"

"Fuck you, Edward."

"Funny, that's the only thing you were really good for." I met her glowering stare for a long moment then started to turn away. "Oh, Sophia," I said, turning back to her with a cold smile on my face and my voice dripping with sarcasm. "Happy eighteenth birthday. Hope it's a special one for you."

Her eyes widened and the scowl on her face was amazing.

I did turn away then. Putting my arm around Marco's shoulders, I led him away from the scene. Neither of us looked back.

Marco was obviously badly shaken and I decided the best thing to do was head back to the car. Anything that we hadn't already bought would have to wait for another day; I needed to get Marco home. The boy didn't speak at all, and I kept my arm around him. I could feel the tension in his body.

I put Marco into the passenger seat and, climbing into the driver's seat, I turned to look at him. His face was pale and I could see that he was on the verge of losing control. Automatically I reached out to him and took him in my arms just as his body started to shake with great wracking sobs.

I held him while he cried, trying to give him what comfort I could. Gradually the sobbing eased, though I still held him against me, his head pressed against my chest. Gently I stroked his hair. "Everything's going to be okay, Marco," I reassured him. On impulse, I pushed his hair back and kissed him lightly on his forehead. "Everything is going to be okay."

Chapter Ten

Marco was very quiet. He didn't speak a single word during the drive back to my apartment, and since we'd got back he'd done nothing but sit in the lounge and stare silently at the TV, a blank look in his eyes. Seeing him like this made my stomach clench, and I silently cursed Helena and Sophia.

How could I ever have believed that I had felt anything at all for Sophia?

I knew I had never loved her; our relationship had been based more on physical need than anything else. But now even thinking about her caused me to feel real disgust. The thought of sex with her now made my skin crawl.

I made myself a coffee and poured Marco his usual glass of juice. Taking these through to the living room, I sat down on the sofa next to the miserable boy and handed him the glass.

"Thanks," Marco said, softly.

"You okay?" I asked him.

He didn't reply immediately, but continued staring at the TV. Then he slowly turned his head to look at me. "She said she didn't even want to see me again. She must really hate me."

"Try not to think about it," I told him. Pretty lame, but I couldn't think of what else to say.

"How can I not think about it? My own mother hates me."

"Well I sure don't hate you," I said. I gave him a smile and put my arm around him. "We can take care of each other; just the two of us. We don't need anyone else."

That got me a smile. Marco looked at me with his big wide eyes. "I love you, Edward."

I was shaken. Not so much by the words but by the sincerity behind them. There was no doubt at all in my mind that Marco did love me, utterly and completely. "I...I love you too," I said, forcing the words out quickly. I knew that I didn't sound convincing, but it was the best I could manage. I still couldn't figure out how I really felt about Marco. *Yes, I did love him; that much was obvious even to me.* There was some kind of bond between myself and Marco. He was special and I felt a need to take care of him and protect him. But what really frightened me was that my feelings seemed to go deeper than that. More than just brotherly affection. My feelings for him were bordering on the sexual, and that was somewhere I wasn't sure I was ready to go.

"I'll tell you what," I said, breaking the sudden tension. "We both need cheering up and we should celebrate you moving in here. How about I do us a special meal?" I glanced at my watch. It was approaching three thirty. There was just time to hurry to the local supermarket, which I knew closed at four on Sundays.

"Yeah, okay."

"Great. Come on. We need to get moving or the shop will be closed." I took Marco's hand and dragged him to his feet and we grabbed our jackets and headed out.

It was a bit of rush, but we managed to get everything we needed: a couple of large steaks, some veggies and buns to go with them, a gooey, creamy, desert type thing that must have contained a heart-attack-inducing number of calories, and a nice bottle of red wine to wash it all down with. By the time we got back, Marco's mood appeared to have improved considerably. Our hectic dash around the shop had left him little time to brood and he now seemed almost back to his normal self.

Having had first hand experience of Marco's complete lack of culinary skills, I decided that his best role in the kitchen would be that of observer. So I had him sit down on one of the chairs, stuck a glass of wine in his hand, and let him offer encouragement from the sidelines while I prepared our dinner.

The meal turned out to be a complete success, both in terms of lifting our spirits and filling our stomachs. The food and the wine had worked like magic, causing us forget about the difficult past and the uncertain future and to just enjoy the present. Even the clearing away, which should have been a chore, was fun as Marco and I joked around, acting like a pair of naughty schoolboys.

Having cleaned up the kitchen and returned to the lounge, I suggested to Marco that he try on some of the new clothes. He'd already tried some of them in the shops, prior to buying them, but I thought it would be nice to see how some of the things went together.

"Sure, why not?" Marco agreed with a grin. He went into the hallway and came back loaded down with bags. He then proceeded to treat me to an impromptu fashion show, modelling a selection of shirts and tops and jeans.

This was a side of Marco that I hadn't seen before: the show-off. Though I suspected that the peek into this aspect of his nature was very much for my eyes only. What was particularly amusing was the repeated partial strip that he made between each change of clothing. He changed in front of me and would undress almost shyly, yet at the same time with a teasing quality to his movements. The overall effect was both sweet and slightly erotic.

"Just get on with it," I laughed as he made a show of slowly unbuttoning the front of a shirt whilst staring me in the eye and running his tongue around his lips.

Marco forced a pout which he managed to hold for several seconds before he too dissolved into laughter. He removed the shirt and laid it carefully aside, selecting a white and blue pullover style top to try on next. He pushed in his arms and was pulling it down over his head when he gave a sudden yelp of pain.

"What's the matter?" I asked, wondering if he had found a stray pin or something.

"I've got it stuck."

"What do you mean, you've got it stuck?"

"It's caught on my earring." Marco had a single, small ring through the lobe of his left ear.

"Oh, okay. Hang on." I got up to look. Leaning in close, I found that a loose thread on the garment had become entangled with the earring. "Don't move; I'll sort it."

"Ow!"

"Nearly got it. Yep, that's it." I pulled the top down over the boy's head, his smiling face appearing through the neck-hole.

"Thanks."

"That's okay."

Neither of us moved.

I stared at Marco's face, just inches away from my own. I could feel my heart pounding and my mouth had gone dry.

Marco's smile disappeared and he looked as scared as I felt.

My gaze went to Marco's sweet-looking, slightly-parted lips. I remembered being here before, and how last time I had lurched back from the precipice at the last moment. I now hovered there on the brink once again, afraid to go forwards, yet at the same time afraid to pull back.

Marco seemed to be begging me with his eyes. His eyes were beautiful, deep pools filled with love and trust. I fell forwards into those eyes, and our lips touched.

It was like a floodgate had been opened. Our lips pressed together firmly, almost frantically. The pressure of the contact forced Marco to take a step backwards, which brought him up against the wall. His arms went around my neck, pulling us even more tightly together. My own hands went to his torso, and to the top, still bunched up around his upper chest. I fumbled lower, seeking out and finding bare skin, and sliding my hands beneath the crumpled folds of the garment. Marco's chest felt warm and silky smooth beneath my fingers, and I could feel his heart pounding hard and fast. I leaned into him, pressing him back against the wall, my mouth on his, my hands exploring his upper body with a firm touch.

"Ughmff!" Marco gave a muffled gasp of pain and I immediately pulled back. "It's okay," he gasped. "Just my ribs are still sore."

"Sorry," I told him, feeling terrible.

He reached out to pull me to him again, but I carefully pushed his hands away. "I'm not sure this is such a good idea," I said, my mind spinning.

"What...?" Marco gave me an anguished, almost panicked look.

"I don't think..."

"Please."

I looked at the boy's face, awash with emotions. I knew instantly that he wanted this more than he had ever wanted anything in his life before. And I knew then, at that same moment, that I wanted it almost as much as he did. "Are you sure?" I asked, knowing that the question was completely unnecessary."

"Oh God, yeah."

I gave him a nervous smile and nodded my own head. "Alright. But let's take things a bit more slowly. I don't want to hurt you."

"You won't." There was complete trust in his voice.

I gave him another smile and then kissed him briefly and lifted the top back up over his head and dropped it to the floor. Marco's lips were once again waiting for mine and our mouths pressed together, my tongue dancing with his. My hands returned to his torso, this time unimpeded by any clothing as I caressed the soft skin of his body. My fingers found one of his nipples; a small protrusion against the otherwise unbroken smoothness of his chest, and I played with it briefly, pinching it between my fingertips and causing the boy to moan softly and squirm deliciously. After a moment I broke off the kiss, my lips working down over his chin and onto his neck where I lightly nibbled at the skin.

Marco's head went back and he gave a groan of pleasure. I moved lower, my lips now nuzzling against the boy's chest, and, finding one of his small nipples, I flicked my tongue across it and then nipped it very gently between my teeth. Marco groaned.

Now his hands were on my head, his fingers tangled in my hair, and he pulled my face more firmly against his slim chest, wordlessly demanding more attention. I released his nipple and continued my downwards journey, over his ribs and his flat stomach, licking his belly button, then down over his completely hairless lower stomach until I reached the belt of his jeans. There, on my knees, I paused.

My heart was thumping at what I was about to do. I felt like a virgin; nervous, inexperienced, not knowing what to expect yet at the same time trembling with tension and barely suppressed excitement. I took hold of the boy's belt and, with shaking hands, I managed to fumble it open. I unfastened the button of his jeans and then stopped and raised my eyes questioningly.

Marco looked down at me and I saw my own fear and excitement mirrored in his eyes. I watched his chest move as he took rapid, shallow, shuddering breaths.

Taking some deep breaths of my own to try to calm myself as I pulled down the zip and watched them spring open to reveal the boxers beneath; the grey shorts I'd lent to him and that I'd worn myself many times before. There was an obvious bulge as the boy's cock pushed at the front of the shorts.

Marco was at least partially hard, and I suddenly realized that I too was in a similar condition.

Rock hard, straining almost painfully inside my jeans.

I quickly reached out and, taking hold of the jeans and boxers at the sides, I pulled them both down together, and as I did so, Marco's cock sprang free, just inches from my face. Marco wasn't quite fully hard, and his slim cock pointed almost straight out, drooping slightly towards the foreskin-covered end. Deliberately, not letting myself think about what I was doing, I wrapped my fingers around the shaft and gave it a squeeze. Marco responded with a soft whimper, and he almost instantly became fully erect in my hand.

This was the first time in my life that I had touched a cock other than my own, and part of my mind flinched away from the idea. My erection, however, responded with a spasmodic throb.

In spite of its hardness, Marco's cock felt velvety warm to the touch and the skin was soft. I released my grip and ran my fingers along the organ, tracing them along the shaft to the point where it widened towards the head. I slowly eased back the skin, watching, with a strange fascination, as it peeled back from the swollen, purple glans.

Moving automatically, I dipped down towards the now exposed head and very light brushed it with my lips in a fleeting kiss.

A shudder passed through Marco's body and he let out his breath in what was almost a sob. I looked up and gave him a smile. He smiled nervously back, and I recalled that he had claimed that he had never done anything with anyone before; this was a first for both of us.

"Let's get these off you," I said, pushing the boy's jeans and boxers all the way down to his ankles. Marco leaned on my shoulders while he removed the last of his clothing; he wasn't wearing any socks. Leaning back on my heels, I looked the eighteen year-old up and down.

This wasn't the first time I had seen Marco naked, or even the first time I'd seen him with a boner, but this was the first time that I'd studied his body in a purely sexual way.

Marco was thin, there was no escaping that, and this gave his body a bony, even angular appearance, but there was a sort of innocence in the way he held himself that was instantly appealing. My gaze travelled up to his face and I saw the boy had been watching me as I appraised his body. He looked down at me, self-consciously, and he had a look in his eyes that told that me more clearly than words ever could that he desperately wanted my approval.

"You're beautiful," I told him, and meant it.

Marco's face lit up, confirming the truth of my words, and he reddened in a blush. He was indeed beautiful.

I got to my feet and leaned into him, my fingers taking hold of his jutting cock, as my lips found his, and we kissed for a long minute. "Maybe I should get undressed," I suggested, giving Marco a grin.

"Okay," he replied, as if happy to go along with anything at all that I suggested. It was obvious that Marco had already fallen into a passive role and was quite happy for, even needed, me to take the lead. I suppose this was to be expected, given his background and the fact that I was older than him, though it did create a problem: I knew nothing at all about having sex with another guy. In fact, before I'd met Marco, the idea had never even crossed my mind. I did, of course, have plenty of experience with girls, and I asked myself how different it could possibly be. Sex was about pleasure. I knew what felt good for guys, being one myself, so I had a good idea about how to make Marco feel good. Besides, if Marco had no previous experience at all, he was hardly likely to criticize. It occurred to me at that point that just as a few moments ago Marco had been seeking my approval, it was equally as important to me that I live up to Marco's expectations. The thought made me smile.

"What's the matter?" Marco asked, noticing my expression.

"Nothing really, it's just that we're both acting like we're scared to death of doing something wrong."

"I am scared," Marco admitted.

"Yeah. Me too."

Marco gave a self-conscious giggle. "We may as well do it wrong together then."

"I guess so." I took a step back and lifted my shirt up over my head, tossing it aside. I could feel Marco's eyes on me as I quickly stripped, and as I stepped out of my silk boxer shorts, his gaze fell on my erect cock.

I was still rock hard.

I moved back towards him, my erection swaying, and his hand tentatively reached out, his fingertips running along the underside of my hard shaft. It felt wonderful. "You sure you haven't done that before?" I groaned.

"Only in my head."

I stood with my hands at my sides, enjoying both the sight and feeling of Marco's fingers exploring my dick. "You've really had fantasies about doing stuff with me?" My vanity made me ask the question.

Marco gave me an embarrassed grin. "Yeah," he admitted, his hand still on my dick. "Almost since the time you first started going out with Sophia; I used to pretend that it was me you were picking up and not her."

"What sort of stuff did you imagine doing with me?" I knew I was being mean asking this, but I couldn't resist.

"Just...stuff. You know what I mean."

"No, that's why I'm asking."

Colour rose in Marco's face and he could no longer look me in the eye. "Sucking and stuff like that," he muttered.

"Me sucking you, or you sucking me?"

Marco squirmed. "Both. But mostly me sucking you."

I put took hold of the boy's chin and lifted it, forcing him to look me in the eye. "You know what?" I told him. "You are so cute when you blush." He tried to look away, but I held him firm and kissed him on the lips. He immediately stopped fighting me and returned the kiss. I put my arms around him and pulled him against me, and he released his hold on my cock, his arms going around my back. Our erections rubbed one against the other as our naked bodies pressed together. After a moment, I moved from his lips and round to the side of his head, nibbling lightly on his earlobe, near the earring. "You want to take this into the bedroom?" I whispered.

"Okay."

I gave him a final quick kiss and then, taking his hand, I led him down the short hallway to my bedroom. He hesitated in the doorway, his eyes flicking nervously between me and the bed. Then he gave a smile and followed me inside.

As we reached the bed, he hesitated again, and this time there seemed to be real fear in his eyes. I sat down on the edge of the bed and pulled him down beside me.

"We don't have to do this," I said to him, gently, keeping hold of his hand. "We can just sit and talk if you want. Or we can get dressed and forget the whole thing." I held my breath, terrified that he was now going to pull back. Even though the idea of what we were about to do scared me, now that I had finally admitted my feelings to myself, I wanted this boy so badly that it hurt.

Marco looked at me and he shook his head. "What if I'm not as good as Sophia?" he asked me, in a cracked voice.

"What?" I asked, incredulously, hardly able to believe that he was even considering this.

"I've heard you tell people how incredible Sophia is in bed. I'm not going to be as good as her."

"Jesus, Marco. You think I'm going to be giving you marks out of ten or something? I don't care how good you are, or how bad you are, or anything like that. I just want us to be together."

"You mean that?"

"Of course I mean it. Come here." I put my arms around him, and as we kissed we toppled over onto the bed. I broke the contact long enough to shuffle onto the bed properly, pulling my number-one boy after me, and then enfolded him in my arms again.

As we kissed, I let my hands explore his body, caressing his shoulders and the smooth skin of his back, his gently curved ass cheeks, then around over his hips to stroke across his balls and rigid cock. From there I moved upwards across his flat stomach and onto his chest, still far more boyish than man-like, my hands wanting to touch him everywhere at once. Marco responded to even the slightest touch, his body squirming and writhing, his breathing ragged and uneven, as though this were something he had been waiting for all of his life. I rolled him onto his back and broke our kiss. He looked at me, a little wild-eyed, but I responded with a grin and very gently nipped his lower lip between my teeth. When I released him, he smiled back at me, nervously. "I love you, Marco," I told him, my voice just a whisper.

The boy's eyes sparkled and he swallowed visibly. Then he pushed against my shoulders and I allowed him to turn the tables, putting me onto my back, surprised that he had suddenly taken the initiative. I was even more surprised when he lifted himself up and sat astride my chest, looking down at me. He paused for a moment and then, with sort of cheeky smile, his hands moved to my shoulders, his fingertips lightly tracing backwards and forwards across my skin. Slowly, he shuffled his body backwards, his concentration intense, as he continued his constantly moving, feather-light touch on my torso. The effect was incredible and it was now my turn to squirm. The contact was maddeningly light yet at the same time amazingly erotic and I was starting to feel as though my body was on fire. As he moved lower, he reached behind himself, bending my erection back and then shuffling down over the top of it so that it was nestled between his ass cheeks, straining to stand upright yet being forced almost painfully downwards. I felt him clench his cheeks and he wriggled his hips backwards and forwards, forcing me to gasp with pleasure as he effectively stroked my cock with his ass. When he then reached behind himself again and fingered the swollen head of my erection, I was unable to hold back a deep groan. And to think that Marco had been worried that he wouldn't be a match for Sophia.

This boy was amazing. I reached out my hand and took hold of his hard cock and Marco gave me a happy grin. While he continued to finger my restrained cock, I played with his erection, stroking and pulling on it. Suddenly, Marco gave a gasp and his cock started to spasm beneath my fingers. I immediately started to pump faster as cum erupted from the head to splash down across my stomach and lower chest. There were four good sized spurts, far more than I had expected, before it slowed to a dribble, and it was an interesting experience for someone who has only ever jerked himself before.

Marco looked at me sheepishly, his breathing heavy. "I'm sorry," he panted. "I couldn't stop it."

"Don't worry," I told him, gently. "It looked like you needed that." I looked down at the smears and splashes of sticky fluid that decorated my stomach.

"Yeah, but... I should have been able to last longer than that."

"It doesn't mean we have to stop," I pointed out. "Unless you want to." And I fervently hoped that he didn't want to; there was no way I could roll over and go to sleep at this point.

"No, I don't want to stop," he said quickly. "I don't ever want to stop," he added with a smile.

"That's my boy!" I gave his now slightly sagging cock another stroke, feeling his sticky cum on my fingers.

Marco let me play with him for a moment and then, pushing my hand away, he climbed off me, and crouched down at my side, taking my erection firmly in his fist. His next move totally amazed me. He leaned forwards and began to lap up his own cum from my stomach.

"Oh, Jesus!" I moaned, as his tongue darted into my belly button. I watched, totally entranced, as he cleaned up every drop of cum from my body, giving me a thorough tongue bath in the process. Even when there was no cum left, his licking continued, moving lower now, nuzzling through my pubes with his tongue and his nose, until I felt that beautiful, agile tongue licking against the base of my erection.

He paused there for a moment and looked up at me, giving another of his cheeky grins, then he once more mounted my chest, this time facing away from me. He bent forwards, dropping his face towards my groin. This presented me with a view of the boy that I hadn't seen before.

Marco's knees were spread wide, on either side of my chest, and as he had bent forwards, this opened up his ass cheeks just inches in front of my face. I found myself staring at his puckered hole, surrounded by a few stray curly hairs. Beneath hung his balls and behind them I could just see the tip of his now soft, sticky cock dangling down. However, before I chance to admire the view, my attention was completely directed to the feelings coming from my groin, as Marco's tongue began swirling around the swollen, exposed head of my hard penis.

"Oh fuck, Marco," I gasped. "That feels fantastic." My hands went to the globes of the boy's ass cheeks, massaging the soft flesh in silent encouragement for him to continue with what he was doing. At any moment I kept expecting to experience the familiar sensation of my cock being enveloped by a warm, willing mouth, but it didn't happen. Instead, the licking continued, all the way around and across the head of my dick, underneath the sensitive rim of my glans, then up and down the shaft. It felt unbelievable.

As Marco continued his licking, my own fingers strayed into the crack of his ass. I knew from some past experiences that being touched and fingered around that area felt good, and I lightly stroked my fingertips over his tightly closed hole. I was rewarded by a muffled groan and the boy squirmed. The groan was repeated as I pressed a little more firmly, right on the hole itself, and Marco pushed his ass back towards me, indicating that he wanted more. I wished I had some sort of lubricant to hand, but there was nothing close by, and I was not about to interrupt things to go looking for some; spit would have to do. I briefly sucked on my fingertip, getting it good and wet and then returned it to the boy's ass, working gently but firmly at that tight entrance, pressing and releasing, frequently rewetting my finger.

Without pausing in his licking, Marco reached back with both of his hands and grasped his ass cheeks, pulling them even further apart.

On impulse, I bent my head forwards and stretched out my tongue to that exposed hole, poking directly at the entrance. A shudder passed through Marco's body and he gave what sounded like a sob.

"You like that?" I asked.

"Don't stop," he begged.

I went at the task enthusiastically, alternately probing at the hole with my tongue and my fingertips, encouraged along in my explorations by the feeling of Marco's tongue which had now extended its range to take in my balls as well as my cock. Gradually, Marco's entrance began to relax and open up until I was able to get the entire tip of my finger inside him. I'd push in, give a little twist and pull back out again and with each twist, Marco would squirm and moan.

Now that I could get my finger inside, I moved my lips further down his ass crack towards his balls, nipping lightly at that sensitive area with my teeth then licking across the back of his balls. A sudden moment of unease passed through me that I was licking a boy's balls; strange how this bothered me, when licking his ass hadn't. Maybe it something to do with the fact that everyone has an ass, but only guys had balls. However, the feeling disappeared as quickly as it had come. It was Marco's ass, and Marco's balls, and Marco's dick, and I wanted him so badly that I was literally aching for him.

I continued to lick on his balls, holding onto them with one hand whilst the index finger of my other hand still probed into the boy's now loosened hole. After a few moments I released Marco's balls and reached under for his dick, which was once more starting to show signs of life. I bent it towards my mouth and nibbled on the boy's foreskin, tasting the sweet stickiness of the pre-cum that was oozing from it. As I nibbled and sucked, I stroked the velvety skin of his shaft, and as it grew to become once more completely hard, I eased the foreskin back and took the entire head of the boy's swollen dick into my mouth. It was a strange sensation and my first experience of sucking cock. A short time ago I would have been disgusted at even thought of doing this, but now, far from feeling any disgust, it was making me feel even more aroused than ever.

As if me taking Marco's cock into my mouth had been a signal, Marco stopped his licking and I felt his warm lips touch the head of my dick and slide slowly down, until he had engulfed the whole of the head and the top part of the shaft. A soft moan forced its way out through my own mouthful of cock. I was in heaven. And just as I thought things could not get any better, I felt Marco's fingers exploring down behind my balls, seeking out my itching ass-hole. I knew then that I couldn't hold back any longer. Marco's mouth around my cock and Marco's fingers probing at my ass were enough to take me over the edge. There wasn't even time to warn Marco what was happening before my cock started to throb and I exploded directly into the boy's mouth.

Marco stiffened and pulled back, giving a choking cough, but, like a true trooper, he went straight back down again, his lips sealing themselves around my shaft, taking my cum into his mouth. Somehow he managed to keep going, swallowing each spurt, not even fazed by my hips thrusting upwards. It was if he were determined to suck out the last drop.

"Marco, you can stop. I'm done," I gasped, squirming as he continued to suck even after I had nothing left to give.

Reluctantly, the boy did finally stop. He sat up and turned around so that he was facing me, and he looked at me worriedly. "Did I do okay?" he asked.

There were smears of cum on his face and a dribble of it running down his chin, and his hair was matted with sweat. He was the sweetest thing I'd ever seen, and I loved him like I had never loved anyone in my life. "Yeah, you did okay," I told him, grinning.

His face lit up in his own grin. "That was pretty awesome," he said.

"It was that, and more besides," I agreed. "But hadn't we better do something about that?" I nodded down in the direction of his still

-rampant erection, which was pointing up towards my face from where he was sitting astride my stomach. "You need to cum again?"

Marco looked down at his erection and then back to me and gave an embarrassed giggle. "Maybe."

I briefly ran my fingers along his shaft, watching it twitch and then moved my hand down to fondle his balls. "Let me watch you jerk it."

"Okay," he gave a shy smile, his shyness seeming out of place considering what he had been doing a few moments ago.

"Shuffle up a bit higher though, so that I can reach you," I told him.

He did as I asked, moving up a few inches so that I could easily reach him with my hands, then he wrapped his fingers around his cock and he started to stroke himself.

I watched for a moment, enjoying the sight of him jerking off in front of me, then I reached out my hand and began to slowly stroke is chest. I found I loved touching him, feeling his soft skin beneath my fingers; it was something I couldn't get enough of. It seemed just moments before Marco was breathing heavily and he was making small thrusting movements. He gave a muffled groan and a spray of sticky fluid flew from his cock. Not the long streamers like the first time he had cum, this time it was more like droplets, most of which splashed down onto my chest.

Marco gave an exhausted smile as he squeezed out the last drops and then he looked sheepishly at the sticky mess on his fingers. His eyes widening in surprise as I took hold of his hand and, pulling it to my own mouth, I licked his fingers clean.

Then, I pulled him down to me, and I kissed him on the lips. "I love you, Marco,"

Marco looked at me and there were tears in his eyes. He lay down beside me, and I held him close.

Sometime later—time had lost meaning—I decided that we'd better clean ourselves up a bit. We took a quick shower together, and I made the most of the opportunity to again get my hands on boy's body as I soaped him up and rinsed him down. Marco seemed to revel in the attention, and obviously enjoyed the contact every bit as much as I did; he even let me dry him afterwards.

Then I suggested that it was time for bed, since I had work the next day, and he had school. He pulled a face, but then gave a nod of reluctant agreement.

It turned out that Marco's school bag was safe in my hall closet; Marco had it put there when he had come over straight from school on Friday, and then, after our row, I had thrown him out without it.

"I'll have to call into work to tell them that I will be a bit late," I told Marco as we towelled off from our shared shower. "I need to pop into the school office when I drop you off. We need to change your address to my apartment seeing as you live here now."

Marco grinned at at that, then his face fell. "But won't they call mum?"

"Possibly." I didn't expect the change to be exactly straightforward, since I was sure they would want some sort of confirmation from Marco's mother, but at least we could set things in motion and we would have to deal with any difficulties as they arose. "One way or another, we'll get it sorted," I told him. "Right, now that we know what we're doing, we'd better get some sleep."

He looked at me, nervously.

I recognized the look that meant he had something on his mind. "What's the matter?" I asked.

"Can I sleep with you, in your bed?"

I put my arms around him and hugged him to me. "I was sort of assuming that we would be sleeping together," I told him. "From now on we can do everything together."

I lay awake for a long time, listening to the soft breathing of Marco as he slept beside me. I was so lucky. In the past couple of weeks, the beautiful young man who lay naked in bed beside me had completely turned my life around in ways that a short time ago I would not even have been able to imagine. I turned my head to look at him, just able to make out his face in the dim light, and I smiled happily to myself.

Marco had taught me so much. He'd taught me to pay attention to the things that really matter, and he'd taught me what love really was. At one time I had thought I'd loved Sophia, but I now realized we'd been nothing more but a convenience to each other. Sophia had used me, but I had also used her. I'd used Sophia for sex, and that was the sum total of our relationship. And that was something else that I'd been wrong about: I'd thought that the sex with Sophia had been good, and, in a way, it had, but only in the physical sense. Sex with Marco went beyond the physical. For the first time in my life I had had sex with someone I cared about, and the difference had been amazing. I now knew that there was far more to sex than simple physical pleasure; there was love. And love was better than anything.

"I really do love you, Marco," I whispered.

Don't miss out!

Visit the website below and you can sign up to receive emails whenever Frank Sol publishes a new book. There's no charge and no obligation.

https://books2read.com/r/B-A-REVY-KJBKC

BOOKS2READ

Connecting independent readers to independent writers.

Also by Frank Sol

Novels Of The Sensual City
A Family Affair

Novels On The Prairies
Bareback Mountain